Aunt Jeanne

Aunt Jeanne

GEORGES SIMENON

, Georges

Translated from the French by
GEOFFREY SAINSBURY

A Helen and Kurt Wolff Book
Harcourt Brace Jovanovich, Publishers
San Diego   New York   London

LC: 82-21539

Library of Congress Cataloging in Publication Data
Simenon, Georges, 1903-
    Aunt Jeanne.
    Translation of: Tante Jeanne.
    "A Helen and Kurt Wolff book."
    I. Title.
PQ2637.I53T313   1983   843'.912   82-21359
ISBN 0-15-109792-5

Printed in the United States of America

First American edition 1983

B C D E

AUNT JEANNE

1

At Poitiers, where she had to change, she hadn't been able to resist the temptation. At least not for long. Ten times, carrying her suitcase, she had passed in front of the refreshment room. The feeling of discomfort in her chest was really agonizing, and it got worse each time she approached her goal. It was like a great bubble of air, certainly quite as big as one of her breasts, which was trying to force its way upward to find an exit, and she waited anxiously, staring in front of her, feeling sure at moments that she was going to die.

She might have a cup of coffee. Yes, just a cup of coffee—she promised herself it would be no more. But at the bar, faced by the waitress with her sleeves rolled up who was washing glasses, she wavered, and, with the blood mounting to her cheeks, she stammered:

"I think I'd better have a little glass of brandy. I'm not feeling well. No doubt it's the heat."

It really was hot, a boiling August day, and the train that had brought her from Paris had been packed with people off for their vacations.

Diffidently, rummaging in her bag for some small change, she muttered:

"Give me another."

It wasn't because of that that she had the impression everybody was looking at her. She'd had just the same feeling a little while earlier in the Paris express. A little boy, sitting between his parents, had stared at her steadily for what seemed an eternity, making her so uncomfortable that she'd had one of her attacks.

It was fatigue. That was all. And advancing years; though not so much the years themselves as the wear and tear they had brought. Yes, she was old and worn out, and hadn't even the courage of an animal to lie down and die.

There had been other women in the train older than she was, dressed in clothes that displayed a large expanse of back and quite a lot of chest, who were off to amuse themselves like teenagers on the beaches of Vendée.

The branch line was served by the same platform as ever, but the little toy train she had known, with high, old-fashioned carriages, had been replaced by a long, silver-painted *micheline,* which glided almost noiselessly through the country, giving only an occasional little hoot as it approached a stop.

She had hoped to arrive after dark, so that she could slink unobserved along the main street. But at seven o'clock the sky was still a luminous blue, tinged with only a little redness in the west. The cows in the fields threw long mauve shadows, and one after the other the windows of the farms reflected a beam of fire as they were caught by the setting sun.

As a child, that hour of the day, fraught with a message of extinction or eternity, had always filled her with awe, reminding her of the purgatory of her catechism; and even now she could see the lime tree outside her bedroom window, each leaf of which was deadly still, as though engraved, and hear the sounds of the house, which seemed to grow louder and louder as the light failed till the mere creaking of a board was enough to rend the silence of the night.

She sucked a peppermint to cover the smell of the brandy, and for the third time since leaving Paris she carefully wiped her face with her handkerchief to remove the last traces of rouge. Originally she had decided not to put any on at all. Only a little powder—perhaps not even that. But at the last minute, fully dressed, she had looked at herself in the glass and been shocked to see a face like a full moon. That was going too far. After all, she musn't frighten them by looking like a ghost, or at any rate as though she had one foot in the grave.

Her dress was just right, plain but dignified, and her hat, considering the price, was in good taste too. Her light summer coat she carried over her arm.

Even in the *micheline* there was nobody she knew, though it was true she hardly dared to look at people for fear of recognizing them. That would have made escape difficult, and she was still looking for a loophole.

"If the Hôtel de l'Anneau d'Or is no longer there, I'll take the night train back to Paris."

Then, because it was a Saturday evening and there were a lot of people on the roads:

"If they've no room left, I won't trouble to look anywhere else."

It was a question of only minutes now, and that horrible feeling in her chest never left her. When the train stopped at the little station, which was almost exactly as it had always been, she hadn't the courage to get up from her seat, because her attack had reached its climax, the point at which she always thought she was going to die. Nevertheless, a moment later, she was standing on the platform. In spite of the daylight, the lights were already switched on. A man in a peaked cap came up and stretched out his hand for her suitcase, saying:

"Taxi?"

She hardly had time to take it all in. In her day there had been no taxis and none of those cars that cluttered up the station yard.

3

"The Anneau d'Or . . ."

The door slammed. She saw a row of houses that seemed surprisingly small, then a street, which they had no sooner turned into than they were at the other end, by the bridge.

"Is that all the luggage you've got?"

She kept her head turned away to avoid being recognized by people in the streets. She was longing to be safely inside the hotel. It must have changed hands. In her day it had been kept by M. and Mme Loiseau. Mme Loiseau, Mathilde, used to wear a wig. They had been over seventy when she had left. As they approached, she had time to notice that a new wing had been built on the right, and it seemed to her that there were more iron tables behind the tubs of laurel that flanked the terrace.

"A single room?"

"Yes."

"Just for the night?"

"Perhaps for a few days."

She didn't know. As a matter of fact, it was highly improbable she'd stay more than one night. Indeed, it was almost inconceivable. But she felt that by such little subterfuges she might disarm a malignant fate.

"Is Number 17 free, Martine?"

"The gentleman's left, but I don't know whether Olga's had time to do the room."

They were young people who couldn't have been married long, and who seemed to be playing at hotel-keeping. It was Madame who called up the stairs:

"Olga! . . . Is Number 17 ready?"

"Yes, Madame."

The visitor filled out the form she was handed. She put her name down as Martineau, of course, Jeanne Martineau, age fifty-seven, born . . .

Born here. Not at the Hôtel de l'Anneau d'Or, but within a hundred yards of it, just across the bridge. She had avoided looking in that direction when she stepped out of the taxi. Would her room, Number 17, look out on the river? Proba-

4

bly not. Not a single room. Besides, on a Saturday night, in August, all the best rooms were sure to be taken.

The old Loiseau couple had, as the local Darby and Joan, been nicknamed Philemon and Baucis. Little did they imagine that a day would come when women would wander about their hotel dressed in nothing but shorts and a brassiere. Mothers of families too! A man stripped to the waist displayed a dark hairy chest and a bright-red shoulder burned by the sun.

"Dinner will be in a quarter of an hour," announced the proprietor—or he might have been only a manager.

He was busy with several things at once, and in the flurry no one thought of Jeanne's suitcase. She dragged it up herself to her room on the third floor. She didn't mind. On the contrary, she was pleased to have made so discreet an entry. The maid, Olga, probably didn't know she was there, or she would have come to see if she needed anything.

The window of Number 17 looked onto the courtyard, where the old stables had now been turned into a garage. The light was failing, the air turning blue, as though smoky. Why shouldn't she go to bed right away? She had some sleeping pills. With three or four, she'd be certain to sleep.

As a matter of habit, she unpacked and put her things away in the wardrobe. Then she washed her face in cold water, after which, without turning the light on, she sat down in the one and only armchair, which was a hard, straight-backed affair, upholstered in the brightest of blues. It looked as if it had never been sat in and reminded her of the furniture displayed in the windows of the big stores.

The minutes slipped by. Gradually night fell. Gradually, too, the sounds from below became more and more distinct, conversation floating upward from the terrace, where people lingered over their *apéritifs* in the evening coolness, and then a fresh series of noises from the dining room when they began to serve dinner. Nearer still, a door slamming, and a shrill, impatient mother threatening heaven knows what if her little boy didn't go to sleep at once. In the background, in spite of passing cars, most of them blowing their horns as they passed, her ears could just detect the thin, almost musical sound of the river, a gentle, friendly sound like a shepherd's pipe, which came from the pier in the middle of the bridge, which divided the water into two streams.

"I'm tired," she said out loud.

The sound of her voice was comforting, and to hear it again she repeated:

"*Mon Dieu,* how tired I am!"

Tired to death. Tired to the point of being ready to sit down on a doorstep, on a curb, on a station platform, anywhere, and just let go, just drift down the stream . . .

She was fat, monstrously fat, so it seemed to her. It disgusted her to have to carry about all that mass of flabby flesh which didn't seem to be part of her real self at all.

A great fat Jaja!

No, she mustn't think of that name, or she would never have the courage. . . .

The darkness of the night rolled in through the window in waves. It frightened her, yet she couldn't summon enough strength to get up from her chair and turn the light on. She simply sat there, bruised and battered, nursing her misery, like someone who can't leave an aching tooth alone. It wasn't merely on account of the two glasses of brandy she'd had at Poitiers that she was disgusted with herself. She was ashamed of being there, of having come back. What had she come for? What was she hoping for?

Because of the discomfort in her chest, she kept her hand pressed to her left breast. It was soft and warm, and little by little an almost voluptuous feeling seeped through her veins. Tears formed on her eyelids and her mouth puckered, like someone's who is on the verge of crying, when in an altered voice she said once again:

"*Mon Dieu,* how tired I am!"

She had fallen asleep where she was, sitting in the armchair, without having taken any pills after all. When she woke up with a start, the sounds in the hotel had died down.

She switched on the crude light from a naked bulb and looked at her watch.

Ten past nine. She was hungry, so imperatively hungry that in the end she went downstairs, stealthily, and crept into the dining room, where half the lights had already been switched off and the two waitresses were laying the tables for the next day.

She walked noiselessly because she always did, because, in spite of her bulk, she wasn't heavy on her feet, but most of all because of her embarrassment. She went up to one of the black-dressed, white-aproned waitresses, who turned around sharply, surprised by her presence, stared hard for a moment, and then burst out:

"Jeanne!"

Adding as though to convince herself:

"Jeanne Martineau!"

The two women looked at each other as though they had something to hide, just as they had at the convent school when one of the nuns was coming.

"You recognized me?"

"Right away. Why? Don't you recognize me?"

"Yes. You're the Hortu girl, only I can't remember your first name."

"Yet you didn't half make fun of it! Désirée . . . But what are you doing here? Have you come to see your brother?"

Jeanne didn't dare ask:

"Is he still alive?"

What she said was:

"Is he here?"

"Of course. A couple of years ago we all thought he was going to be the next mayor. Then something cropped up at the last minute and spoiled his chances."

They suddenly realized that they were standing in the middle of the dining room, one of them a waitress, the other a guest.

"Is there something you wanted? Are you staying in the hotel?"

"Yes. I've had no dinner. I'm hungry."

7

"I'll see about that. You're too late for the full menu, of course, but there's bound to be something left, and they'll only charge you for what you have. Will that do?"

"Perfectly."

"You'd better sit here. If I brought it up to your room, the skinflint would want to put it on the bill. They don't give anything away here. They're Paris people, who've just taken over the place, and you can see they don't really know this kind of business. . . . What would you like?"

"Anything."

"The roast beef's off, but I could get you some ham and potato salad. If you'd like some soup—but I warn you it's pretty poor stuff. . . . Did you hear of Julien's accident?"

Jeanne almost repeated the name uncomprehendingly. Then she remembered she'd had a nephew, whose name she'd forgotten, who would now be grown up.

"Poor fellow," went on Désirée. "He was the best of the bunch. I'm sorry."

"That's all right. Go on."

"To go and get killed like that! And at a place he knew like the palm of his hand and where never a month passes without an accident . . . You know—that bend in the road at Loup Pendu, just after the mill. . . . He had his wife in the car with him too. It's a miracle she didn't have a miscarriage. The child was born prematurely, it's true, but the doctors managed to save it. . . . Didn't you know?"

"No . . . At least . . ."

"I'll be back in a minute."

How long ago was it? . . . Let's see. She was fifty-seven now and she'd left the convent before she was eighteen. . . . Had she seen Désirée since then? She might have run into her by chance during the years that followed. Two or three times, perhaps. She really couldn't be sure. The Hortus had a farm some way from the town, and the girl had never been a close friend of hers.

Say, roughly forty years . . . Yet they had recognized each other. Jeanne could have sworn Désirée's voice and way of speaking were exactly the same as ever. Moreover, they had quite naturally slipped at once into the easy intimacy of schoolgirls, as though they had never lost sight of each other.

She had taken her friend so much as a matter of course that she hadn't even thought of asking by what strange set of circumstances the daughter of a prosperous farmer had become a waitress at the Anneau d'Or.

"I've got a few sardines and some radishes here. You can start in on them. You'd like some wine, I suppose. . . . Red? White? It's probably been bought at your brother's."

She didn't seem in the least unhappy. She was thin and flat-chested, with no hips behind her apron. That was strange, because at the convent she had been the fattest girl of the class, very self-conscious about her enormous arms and legs.

"Will you be staying here for some time?"

"I don't know yet. I don't suppose so."

"Have you any children?"

Jeanne shook her head.

"Sorry if I said the wrong thing. I've had three, but I lost two."

She said it as a simple statement of fact.

"My daughter and her husband live in Algeria. He's a hard-working man, her husband, and I'm sure they'll do well. . . . I'll just finish laying the tables, then we can have a good talk."

They weren't able to, and Jeanne was rather relieved, though she couldn't have said why. She had been desperately hungry before, but she ate without appetite, watching the two waitresses going to and fro in the murky, backstage light. From time to time Désirée gave her a friendly nod and when she brought the plate of ham she whispered:

"Be quick. I don't want them to see I've given you three slices."

A little later, the proprietress, or, as Désirée called her, the skinflint, came into the room.

"Have you finished, Désirée?"

9

"In a moment. I just have to bring Madame's dessert and coffee."

"Emma can see to that. You're wanted in the office."

Before leaving the room, Désirée was just able to whisper:

"She reminds me of the Mother Superior. Do you remember? . . . I'll be seeing you again."

The skinflint had left the door open between the dining room and the café, and Jeanne could hear the clack of billiard balls and the voices of the card players, while wisps of pipe and cigar smoke, laden with the smell of beer and spirits, drifted in toward her table.

It was that smell that tempted Jeanne. She couldn't put it down to her chest this time, since she was feeling no discomfort at all. She didn't put up a struggle. She might have had some compunction in asking Désirée, but Emma, who was now looking after her, was young and a stranger.

"Do you think I could have a glass of cognac?"

"I'll send you the waiter."

And she shouted through the doorway:

"Raphäel! A cognac."

He came in with the bottle. He was young too, fair and curly, looking rather awkward in a waistcoat that had previously been worn by someone of a much more portly build.

"Just a moment, young man," said Jeanne in a different voice, a little husky, as she lifted her glass to drain it at a draft.

And as she held her glass out, she went on familiarly:

"The same again. One can't walk on one leg."

She said it with a vulgar chuckle, but repented at once. Indeed she was so ashamed of herself that, alone in the dining room, now ready for the next meal, she almost left the second glass untouched. She even got up to go, but at the last moment she snatched up the drink and practically flung the stuff down her throat.

She heard the bells ringing for early mass and could recognize those of the two parish churches and the thinner high-pitched ones of the infirmary for old people. The maid had hurried in with her breakfast on a tray, and from every side came the sounds of doors slamming, taps running, and plugs being pulled.

She felt less brave than ever in the bright morning light that flooded her yellow-painted room, and she stayed late in bed, then dawdled over dressing. She thought of Désirée, wondering if she slept in the hotel. If she did, it would probably be in one of the little rooms over the garage. Could she ask her to come and see her?

From her she had learned that Julien was dead, that he'd been married, and that his wife had had a baby, but she had practically no news of any of the others. Of course Désirée would take it for granted she knew. But Jeanne knew nothing. On her arrival she hadn't even known whether her brother was living or dead.

All that had reached her—and that was during the time when she still corresponded occasionally with her family—was the news of her brother's marriage to Dr. Taillefer's daughter, Louise, who had been at school with her too, though in a much younger class, so that Jeanne could only vaguely remember a dark little thing with a sharp nose and brazen eyes and two pigtails down her back.

What would she be like now? She must be already in her fifties, like Robert. The latter must certainly have become stout; he had had the tendency even as a boy.

Jeanne powdered her face, wiped it, then powdered it again. Then, seeing her complexion white as a sheet, she put a little rouge on her finger and lightly smeared it over her cheeks. The effect was slightly mauve. It always was—she didn't know why. She had tried every tint of rouge, but it always seemed to turn slightly mauve when she came to use it.

"An old clown," she said to herself.

There was no use spending the whole day trying to pluck up her courage. The only thing was to take the plunge. She had come thousands and thousands of miles to get here, and now all she had to do was cross the bridge and walk straight up to the big double doors that opened onto the courtyard

11

inside, in one of which a wicket was inserted. In the old days the doors had been painted dark green. Her father had always insisted on bottle green. For the shutters too. The house itself was white, but a rich, soft, creamy white, quite different from the cold white of the other houses. She had only to lift the brass knocker and the sound would echo under the vault of the entrance like a peal of bells.

She would hear steps. A man? A woman? A silly question. Obviously it would be the maid who'd open the door, a maid who wouldn't know her, and who, if she was properly trained, would ask:

"What name shall I say?"

And there she was. She had taken the plunge. She had crossed the bridge, gone up to the dark-green door, lifted the knocker, and let it fall. As it echoed, she read on the long blind wall of the warehouse: ROBERT MARTINEAU. VINS EN GROS, and the words were borne out by a row of empty casks on the sidewalk. Only the name had changed. In the old days it had been LOUIS MARTINEAU, that being her father's name. Lastly there was the same old notice prohibiting the posting of bills: *Défense d'Afficher.*

A voice inside called out:

"Alice! There's somebody at the door."

"I know. But I can't come down now."

Light, hurried steps. A bolt shot back. A slender woman all in black, with her hat and gloves on and her missal in her hand.

"Were you going out?" asked Jeanne automatically.

"No. I've just got back from church. . . . What is it?"

She seemed agitated, nervous, perhaps anxious. So far, she hadn't even had the curiosity to look her visitor in the face.

"I suppose you're Madame Martineau, Robert's wife?"

"Yes."

"I thought I could recognize you. We were at school together, only you were a good deal younger than me."

It looked as though the other, with her own thoughts gnawing at her, was hardly listening.

"I'm Jeanne Lauer."

"Ah!"

She hesitated, like someone who doesn't know what to do with a cumbersome parcel.

"Come in," she said at last. "But I'm afraid you'll find us in an awful mess. My maid walked out on me yesterday without so much as a day's notice. I managed to get hold of another girl, who was to have come this morning. But she doesn't seem to have turned up. I can't think where Robert's got to. I've been looking for him for the last five minutes."

She pushed open a door and called out:

"Robert! Robert! Your sister's here."

Then, as a thought seemed to strike her:

"Is your husband with you?"

"He died fifteen years ago."

"Oh! . . . Julien's dead too. Did you know?"

"I heard about it yesterday."

"So you were here yesterday?"

"I arrived in the evening. I thought it was too late to disturb you."

Her sister-in-law let the matter drop. She took off her hat and gloves and went through the rooms, which, to Jeanne, were hardly recognizable. All sorts of changes had been made. They were furnished differently, and even the smell had altered.

"I can't imagine where Robert's stowed himself away. I left him just to go to mass, asking him to look after the new servant if she came while I was out. Since we needed someone in a hurry, I telephoned an agency in Poitiers, and they promised to send me someone by the first train in the morning. She should have been here long ago. . . . Robert! Robert! . . . I'm so sorry to be receiving you like this. The whole house is upside-down, and I don't know when we'll ever get it straight again!"

A young woman, also dressed in black, leaned over the banister.

"What is it?" she asked, without seeing Jeanne.

13

"Robert's sister. Your Aunt Jeanne, who's been living in South America . . . It is South America, isn't it? I'm not sure—it's so long since we . . . Alice! You haven't seen Robert, have you? I've looked in the office. He's not there."

"Is the office still on the other side of the yard?" asked Jeanne.

"Yes. Why? You haven't heard him go out, have you, Alice?"

"I'm sure he hasn't. I'd have heard the door shut. I think I heard him go upstairs. . . . Ah! There we are again!"

The piercing screams of a baby came from one of the second-floor rooms, and Louise winced, as though from a sudden stab of neuralgia.

"Don't judge me too harshly, Jeanne. You probably think I'm crazy. Oh, yes, you do. I can see it in your eyes. And sometimes I wonder myself whether we're not all a bit crazy here. But how can I be expected to cope single-handed with a huge house like this? Maids leave, one after the other. The last one simply walked out without saying a word. It was after lunch yesterday. I noticed that the table hadn't even been cleared, let alone the washing up done, and when I went up to her room I found she had packed her things and flitted. . . . The baby shrieks the whole day, and it won't be long before his mother goes out, leaving him on my hands. She says a girl of her age can't stay boxed up indoors all the time. As for my daughter, I haven't the faintest idea where she is, and Henri went off last night, taking the car with him. . . . If only Robert . . ."

She was obviously on the verge of tears. At any moment now she might slump down in a chair and start sobbing. But no. Once again she started calling out:

"Robert! . . . Robert!"

Her nerves were all on edge. She started up the stairs, looking tiny in that spacious house. Her daughter-in-law put her head around a door to snap:

"How on earth do you expect me to get the baby to sleep with you shouting all over the place?"

14

"There you are, Jeanne! Did you hear that? It's all my fault for shouting! Whatever happens, I'm the one who's to blame!"

She pulled herself up.

"I haven't even asked you to sit down," she went on, "or offered you anything. The truth is I'm worried about Robert. It's strange he doesn't answer. I'm sure he hasn't gone out. He never goes out without a hat, and his hat's hanging in the hall. He's not in the office or the cellars. In any case he has nothing to do there on a Sunday. Come up, Jeanne. I daresay you'd like to wash your hands."

Even the treads of the stairs had been replaced, for they no longer creaked. The woodwork, formerly grained and varnished, was now painted white, the walls distempered in pale colors. In her room, Louise threw her hat onto the unmade bed, then stooped to pick up a man's pajamas that were lying on the carpet.

"I hate you to see the house like this, but I can't help it. There are times when everything seems to be against me. . . . If only I knew where Robert was . . ."

She started up the stairs to the third floor, where the children's rooms used to be and an attic that had been converted into a playroom. Jeanne remained below, but could hear her opening and shutting one door after another, calling out each time:

"Robert!"

Two doors, three doors, four doors.

"Robert! . . . Robert!"

She reached the attic at the end of the passage, threw open the door, and called out more shrilly than ever:

"Robert!"

And the next moment:

"Jeanne! Alice! Help! . . . Quick!"

A small black figure, she cowered against the whitewashed wall, her shoulders hunched, her fist thrust into her mouth.

The light, as formerly, came blazing in through a large

15

skylight, which had been set into the sloping roof, and which could be opened by means of a rod that hung down into the room.

There had been a time when Jeanne had had to stand on a stool to reach that rod, and then a time when she could just reach it standing on tiptoe. Above the skylight a big hook was fixed to a joist, the sort of hook you see at a butcher's. No one had ever known what it was there for.

It was to that hook that Robert had fixed a rope and hanged himself.

Jeanne had guessed right. He had grown fat, as fat as she was, perhaps more so. He was wearing a suit of fine, smooth cloth, but still had on the felt slippers in which he liked to mooch around on a Sunday morning. At least he had one on. The other had fallen onto the floor.

An empty box, which had served as a platform, had been kicked aside. Near it on the floor lay a sheet of paper on which a single word had been scribbled in blue pencil:

Pardon.

With her fist thrust further and further into her mouth, Louise was turning purple, as if she were suffocating. From below came Alice's voice:

"What's the matter? Do you really want me?"

"Bring up a glass of cold water," Jeanne called back, astonished at the firmness of her own voice.

As an afterthought, she added:

"And a knife . . . Or some big scissors might do. . . . Quick!"

The baby was screaming again. Louise looked at her sister-in-law with the eyes of a frightened animal.

Robert's body swung slowly from side to side at the end of the rope, one shoulder curiously twisted. The beam of sunshine just caught that shoulder, then passed on to throw a rectangle of light on a dappled gray rocking horse that had lost its mane, but whose bright china eye was fixed on the dead man.

2

Every detail was stamped on her memory, every attitude, every movement, though not necessarily in the correct order. To start with, she could of course clearly remember lifting the knocker, standing in the sun, a treacly, ten-o'clock-in-the-morning, Sunday sun; and at that moment she was a broken-down old woman who couldn't go on any longer, who sued for mercy, who felt like a stray dog cringing at a farmhouse door, knowing well it was more likely to get a kick than a bone. And if anything, she had felt worse still, emptier, more utterly forlorn, when a little later she had gone panting up the stairs in the wake of her sister-in-law, who was leading her heaven knew where.

But why, when Alice brought up the glass of water, had Jeanne thrown it into Louise's face instead of giving it to her to drink? She had done it unthinkingly, suddenly disgusted by Louise's convulsed features or by the sound of her nails digging into the plaster wall.

As for the other, the daughter-in-law, she wasn't much use

either. She seemed to have nothing on under her black dress—she probably hadn't—and she had neither washed nor fixed her hair. She held her left hand up to shut out the spectacle, while with the other she held out a kitchen knife, beating a retreat as soon as Jeanne had taken it, merely excusing herself with:

"I can't stay in the same room as a dead person—I simply can't."

"Well, you can at least telephone for a doctor."

"Dr. Bernard?"

"Any doctor. The one who'll come quickest."

Presumably Alice did so. She must have rushed right down to the ground floor without stopping to see to the baby, for the latter went on screaming at the top of its voice. After her telephone call, which, as Jeanne realized later, she had to make from the dining room, she didn't stay indoors, but went out and waited for the doctor on the sidewalk.

The expression on Louise's face when she got the splash of cold water was one of almost comic astonishment; then a sudden spark of hatred flashed from her eyes, as from those of a child who has received a slap. She didn't go away at once. For a minute or two she must have stayed there crouching against the wall. It was only when Jeanne, after laying Robert's body on the floor, turned around, opening her mouth to speak, that she found she was alone.

She was absolutely calm. What decisions she took, she took without reflection, without effort. It was as though all her actions had been predestined. In a corner of the attic, half concealed by a stack of books, was an old mirror flecked with mold in a black-and-gold frame. She fetched it, noticed that it was much heavier than one would expect, so much so that she had some difficulty in holding it in front of her brother's mouth.

At that moment, she heard approaching steps, swift steps, but solid, reassuring, masculine ones, while a voice said:

"I'll find my way up. You see to the baby."

It was then that the name she had heard a few minutes

before struck a chord in her memory and became incarnate. In the old days, a man named Bernard had worked for many years in her father's cellars, though for some mysterious reason the children had always called him Babylas. He was very short and fat and had a bulbous nose, and always wore extremely baggy trousers that made his legs look even shorter than they were. Now that she came to think of it, Babylas had been the name of a pig dressed up as a man that they'd seen in a circus.

He lived on the outskirts of the town, near the Chêne Vert, and had six or seven children, one of whom would often come to fetch him after the day's work.

As soon as she saw the doctor, she was sure he was one of those children; in fact, his first name was on the tip of her tongue. He must have been only a little boy when she left town.

"I think he's dead, Doctor. I thought I ought to cut him down. I'm afraid his head banged on the floor, when he slipped out of my arms, but I don't suppose it's made any difference."

He was in his early forties and, unlike his father, he was tall and slim, though he had just the same fair hair. As he put down his bag and knelt by the body, she ventured to question him, though he hadn't spoken to her, hadn't even looked at her when he came in.

"You're Charles Bernard, aren't you?"

The name had just come back to her. The doctor nodded and threw a swift glance at her as he put his stethoscope to his ears.

"I'm his sister, Jeanne," she explained. "I got here only this morning. That is, I arrived in town last night, but didn't want to bother them, so I spent the night at the Anneau d'Or."

It was only then that it struck her that, if she'd come straight around the evening before, she'd have found her brother alive. By association of ideas, her mind went back to the hotel dining room, Raphäel standing in front of her with the bottle, and the two glasses of cognac that had made her feel so guilty.

"There's nothing to be done," stated the doctor, getting up. "He's been dead for the last hour."

"I suppose he came up as soon as my sister-in-law went to church."

The baby's cries hadn't stopped. A slight frown came to the doctor's forehead as he glanced out through the door.

"It was Louise who found him," she explained. "It must have been a terrible shock."

"We'd better go down. Do you know if he left any message?"

Only a corner of the sheet of paper was showing, the rest being under the body. Jeanne managed to pull it out, however, allowing him to read that one word, scribbled in large letters: *Pardon.*

The doctor's attitude didn't strike her at once. It was difficult to think clearly with that horrible noise going on. For the baby's crying was positively painful. It seemed to fill the whole house and echo against every wall.

Charles Bernard was obviously a cool and collected man whose movements would always be measured and who would certainly be guarded in the expression of his feelings. He was nonetheless a Bernard, who had known the whole family, had played in the yard as a boy, and hidden behind the casks. Yet he hadn't seemed in the smallest degree surprised that Robert Martineau should have hanged himself in the attic. On seeing the brief message the dead man had left, he hadn't moved a muscle. If he had reacted at all, it was merely to become a shade graver, like a man who sees the accomplishment of what has for long been inevitable.

Had he even been surprised to find Alice on the sidewalk? Or to find someone else instead of Louise by the dead man's side?

"We'd better go," he repeated.

On the second floor, without even knocking, he barged straight into the room from which the cries were coming. The mother was lying face downward on the unmade bed, her face buried in the pillow, her fingers pressed to her ears, while the baby, clutching the bars of its crib, was shrieking for all it was worth.

Without a moment's hesitation, Jeanne picked it up and held it against her shoulder. Little by little the cries grew fainter, gave place to a gurgle or two, and then to sighs.

"You don't think he's ill, do you, Doctor?"

"He wasn't the last time I came, which was three days ago, and I see no reason why he should be now."

The unaccustomed absence of the cries brought the mother back to life. She turned her head, showing an eye between her tousled hair and the pillow. The next moment she sprang lithely to her feet, shaking her head to throw her hair back from her face.

"I must apologize, Doctor. I know I'm a bad mother. People never stop telling me so. I just can't help it. That crying simply drives me mad. Just now, when I came back into the room, I could almost have bashed its head against the wall. It's been going on ever since first thing this morning, and I've tried everything. . . ."

She looked at Jeanne with a surprise tinged with suspicion.

"You see! As soon as he's in someone else's arms, he's all right. That's what I've been telling you all along, only you wouldn't believe me. He's got no use for his mother!"

Jeanne's and the doctor's eyes met, and they both felt slightly embarrassed, as though they already were in some subtle way in league with each other.

"Where's your mother-in-law?"

"She went downstairs, then came up again. For a while I heard her moving around, opening and shutting doors. Now I think she's locked herself in her room, which means we won't see anything of her for the next few hours."

They seemed to understand each other perfectly, to be speaking of everyday things, things, at any rate, that were in no way strange or exceptional and needed few words to explain them.

"Were you in the house when your father-in-law went up to the attic?"

"Yes. I was in here. I heard him go upstairs, in spite of the baby's crying. He's been crying ever since his first bottle this morning, though I swear I gave him the right amount. Of course I didn't take any notice—of Robert, I mean. Then my mother-in-law came back from church and started calling him. Then there was a knock on the front door and . . ."

She looked at Jeanne, not knowing quite what to call her. Madame would have been out of place. She didn't quite dare to call her by her first name, and as for Aunt Jeanne—well, she hadn't yet got used to the idea of her being a relation.

". . . and *she* arrived. . . ."

"I shall have to notify the police."

"Why? Since he killed himself . . ."

"I've no choice. I'd better call up from here and wait for the inspector; he'll want to see me."

"There's a telephone in my mother-in-law's room. But of course . . ."

She stopped.

"I was forgetting she'd locked herself in."

"I'll go downstairs. Don't bother. I know where the telephone is. Meanwhile I'd be grateful if you could persuade Madame Martineau to have a word with me."

He said nothing to Jeanne, who followed him down, still carrying the baby, who was now quite happy and half asleep. Neither she nor the doctor thought it in the least odd that she should accompany him. It was he who led the way. The house was so changed that she hardly knew where she was. It was not only the furniture. Walls had been pulled down and others built.

She was still wearing her hat. It was only in the dining room that she finally pulled it off with one hand, without disturbing the baby, and put it down on the table.

"Hello? Police? Is that you, Marcel? . . . I suppose the inspector's not in this morning. Do you know where I could get hold of him? . . . Dr. Bernard speaking."

It was curious to hear the little Bernard boy of former

days, whom Jeanne had known in short pants cut from his father's old trousers, now speaking in a voice of quiet authority. He was probably married and living in a comfortable modern house. Yes, he was almost certainly a family man, and no doubt Alice's telephone call had found him surrounded by his children, with whom he had just returned from mass.

"Thanks. I'll see if I can get him."

And he calmly asked for another number.

"Madame Gratien? This is Dr. Bernard. . . . Yes, thanks, and you? Is the inspector there? . . . Do you think I could have a word with him? I'm sorry to disturb you, but it's important. . . . Thank you. I'll hold on."

Still holding the receiver to his ear, he turned around to speak to Jeanne, and for the first time he seemed to make some personal contact with her. Why should she have been so impressed? Not that there was anything peculiar either in his voice or in the way he looked at her. Nor did he put any special emphasis on his words to hint at anything. What he said was quite simple; yet it seemed, on that occasion, to be of exceptional importance. There was a lot behind the words—of that she felt sure, and she was equally sure he would read into her answer far more than the mere words conveyed.

In itself it was a commonplace enough remark.

"Will you be staying here for some time?"

"I don't know yet. In fact, when I came this morning I hadn't the faintest idea."

She hesitated, and then went on:

"Was my brother a bit worn out too?"

He didn't have time to answer, because the inspector had come to the phone, having been fetched from the end of the garden, where he was fishing in the river.

"Hello, Hansen! Bernard here . . . Fine, thanks . . . I'm calling from the Martineaus'. Robert Martineau has hanged himself. . . . Yes, he's dead. He'd been dead for some time when I came. There was nothing to be done. You see, with all that weight, one of the cervical vertebrae fractured. . . .

Yes, I'd prefer it, if you can manage it. . . . Right. Then I'll expect you in about twenty minutes. Meanwhile, I'll start on my report."

Jeanne didn't repeat her question, which now seemed superfluous. The doctor didn't come back to it either. The baby was fast asleep, red in the face. Only now and again was there a catch in its breath.

"I think you'd better try to persaude Madame Martineau to open the door."

"Are you afraid of something happening?"

He didn't answer that question either, but he didn't appear to be anxious. All he said was:

"The inspector will certainly want to see her. He couldn't very well do otherwise."

The door to the kitchen was open, like most of the doors in the house, and the doctor seemed suddenly to notice the silence there, for he asked:

"What about the maid? Isn't she here?"

"It seems she walked out of the house yesterday without saying a word to anybody. They were expecting another girl this morning, but she hasn't appeared yet."

No comment. He fished his case book out of his bag and slowly unscrewed the cap of his fountain pen as he sat down at the corner of the table to make his notes.

"I daresay you could put the baby back in its crib now without waking it. Anyhow, you might try. He's a heavy boy."

For the second time, she went upstairs, slowly and carefully, holding one shoulder higher than the other, on account of the baby, whose moist warmth she could feel against her body. She didn't bother to knock on Alice's door, but went straight in, to find her leaning out the window looking down onto the quay, smoking a cigarette, her thin dress clinging to her thighs. The smoke of her cigarette hung in her hair.

Jeanne cautiously laid the baby down in its crib. Hearing her, Alice turned around to say disagreeably:

"Had enough of him, haven't you? Now he'll start crying again worse than ever."

give her my condolences and tell her that I'll do all in my power to reduce the necessary formalities to a minimum."

"Must the body remain where it is?"

"No. We're quite satisfied it was suicide. In all probability we can even dispense with a post-mortem. You can get the undertaker in at once; in fact"—he threw a sidelong glance at the steaming cup she was wiping—"in fact, considering the time of year, you oughtn't to delay a moment."

The doctor was standing behind him. He seemed quite unmoved, a calm spectator of all that went on.

"I don't think your sister-in-law will need me today. If she does, however, you can get me at any time at my home."

And she answered quite simply:

"Thanks."

It was half past eleven when the undertaker arrived with two men. For form's sake she went and knocked at Louise's door, but got no answer. She hadn't thought of taking her apron off, and her hands smelled of onions.

"I think the best thing would be to lay him out in the blue room," she said after a rapid glance at the rooms on the second floor.

Alice, who was standing near, grumbled:

"That's Mad's room."

"Then what about the next one?"

"That's Henri's."

"Well, one of them will have to go upstairs. We can't leave the body up there."

"You can arrange that with them. As far as I'm concerned, I'll find somewhere else to sleep tonight."

Jeanne made no answer, and the undertakers brought the body down to the blue room and shut themselves in.

On the other side of the bridge, a broad streamer was stretched across the street. Groups of people had gathered on the sidewalks. On that bright sunny morning, every detail stood out sharply. The terrace of the Anneau d'Or was crowded, and, glancing through an open window, Jeanne had a glimpse of Raphäel's curly hair, as he darted in and out among the tables. There was a bicycle race on, and a loudspeaker had just announced that the leading competitors were just coming over the brow of the hill.

"Where's Madeleine gone?" asked Jeanne.

"Do you imagine she takes me into her confidence?"

"When did she go?"

"This morning, just before the baby woke up. It must have been about six."

"Was she alone?"

"Of course not. Some people called for her in a car. I heard the horn, and a moment later she came down."

"Who were they?"

"Friends."

"What friends?"

"Boys. That's all I can tell you. If you want to know more, you can ask her when she comes back. She must have been in shorts, because all her dresses are in her wardrobe."

"Is there any chance of her getting back early?"

"More likely tomorrow morning. I wouldn't mind betting they've gone swimming at Royan."

"And her brother?"

"You heard what his mother said, didn't you? Once again, Henri's gone off with the car. I don't know how he managed to get hold of the ignition key, since his father always kept it hidden."

"How old is he?"

"Nineteen."

"And Madeleine?"

"Imagine you being their aunt and not knowing! Though of course it's true you've . . ."

She bit her lip. Not that she was embarrassed. On the contrary, she made it quite obvious.

"True I've what?"

"Nothing. Anyhow, it's no business of mine. Am I right in supposing you've come back to live here?"

She looked at Jeanne's blue apron, which made it so obvious that she didn't wait for an answer, but just went on:

"And if you want to know about me, I was twenty last week, and I lived just five months with Julien. Perhaps you understand what that means."

"There's the baby waking."

"That's right! The baby! Always the baby! And since you're so successful with him, perhaps you'll go and see to him."

"I'm going down to finish getting his food ready. Meanwhile you'll look after him yourself. Do you understand?"

She had never been so calm in all her life, and Alice, taken aback, couldn't find anything to answer. It was only when Jeanne was on the stairs that she made a face at her behind her back. Then, lighting another cigarette, she slouched back to the baby.

Jeanne opened the oven door, and the sizzling of the fat as she basted the roast was like music to her ears, a sound as proper to a kitchen as the chirping of crickets is to the fields at night. On top of the stove, the lids of the saucepans trembled as the steam escaped.

"That's right! Start howling again, you little beast! As soon as your mother comes near you, off you go. If you don't shut up, I'll hand you over to Aunt Jeanne again."

Aunt Jeanne didn't raise her eyebrows, didn't even smile. With a corner of her apron she wiped her forehead, which was beaded with sweat.

The undertaker appeared with a notebook in his hand.

"I quite understand the situation, and I'm very sorry to bother you. . . . It's about the list. . . ."

She didn't understand.

"There'll be a lot of notices to send out, because Monsieur Martineau was very well known and highly respected throughout the district. I can get the business acquaintances from the chief clerk tomorrow morning. For the rest . . ."

"I'll speak to my sister-in-law about it presently."

"Ask her not to delay. As for the religious question . . ."

"Did my brother go to church?"

31

"No. I don't think so. But he was undoubtedly a man of Christian principles."

He was a young man, who did his utmost to play the part well, looking as solemn as he could. He added:

"I'm convinced Madame Martineau would wish for absolution."

"Is it possible? I thought the Church, in cases of suicide, refused all . . ."

"Excuse me, but I know all about it. In principle, what you say is quite right, but in practice they're not as rigid as all that. Particularly if the deceased was of unsound mind at the moment. In that case they'll do what they can. Even in other cases, if death doesn't supervene immediately, they can assume full and complete repentance. That makes all the difference, and even a few seconds may be enough. . . . Excuse my going into such technical details. If you allow me, I'll sound out the priest privately and let you know what view he takes."

"Thank you."

She forgot to show him out and he found his way to the door, where the two other men were waiting for him. Only when they had gone did she remember that the door had always been bolted inside, and she went and saw to it.

Coming back into the kitchen, she was for the first time conscious of her back. It was aching and her limbs were heavy. For a moment or two she stood in the middle of the room, not knowing what to do with herself. To one side of her was a shelf on which was a row of spices and condiments used for cooking. Among them stood a bottle with Madeira in gold letters on the label, and Jeanne was seized by a sudden impulse, which she checked only just in time. Her mind went back to the bar on the station platform at Poitiers, and the fair, curly-haired Raphäel, then to Désirée in the half-lit dining room of the Arneau d'Or, saying in her monotonous, matter-of-fact voice:

"I've had three children, but I lost two. . . ."

And her room, in which she had lingered as long as possible, stewing in her own juice, listening to the sounds of the hotel and the street, doors opening and shutting, faucets running, plugs being pulled, women in shorts coming and going, children being scolded, passing cars . . .

It was the first time in ages that her back had actually ached. But then, she was no longer used to all this running up and down stairs. Perhaps it was the cumulative effect of the hours she had spent in the train, and before that in the ship. They had been through some bad weather, and she had been seasick. Six in a third-class cabin. She hadn't stopped in Paris, but had staggered blindly on, not knowing why, not knowing what she expected or even what she hoped for, only conscious of one thing—that, if she once paused, she'd never have the courage to go on again.

She was tired. God! She was tired. And her legs were swollen as they always were when she did too much. Only, up to then, she hadn't had time to notice it that morning. Or that her feet were hurting. No wonder they did, since she'd had her new shoes on all the time, the ones she'd bought specially to come here.

Screams from the baby. That brought her back to her duties. And that twenty-year-old Alice, who was leaning over the banister to shout down from the second floor:

"I thought you said you'd get his food ready!"

With a movement that was already becoming automatic, she wiped her forehead again with the corner of her apron, smiled vaguely, and answered, as she fetched a bowl from the cupboard:

"It'll be ready in a moment. I'm coming."

3

It must have been about two o'clock when the sun disappeared behind the clouds, and it was at the same moment that three or four sudden gusts of wind swept through the windows, bellying curtains and slamming doors, after which the air was still and oppressive, remaining so right up to the first rumbling of thunder a good deal later in the afternoon.

The gusts of wind coincided with Alice's departure, and, on account of the noise they occasioned, Jeanne didn't realize till the last moment what was afoot. The young mother hadn't said anything further about her revulsion against sleeping in a house where there was a corpse, and anyone might have thought her words were an empty threat, made under the influence of the shock they had all received that morning.

Sitting on the edge of the unmade bed, over which, however, she had thrown a bedspread, with her legs crossed and her hair falling over her face, she had watched Jeanne feed the baby, with her thoughts apparently far away. After a while she had become a little more human.

Jeanne had remarked:

"He's my great-nephew, yet I don't even know his name."

"At first the idea was to call him Julien after his father, but I couldn't bear him to be named after someone who'd come to a violent end. I'm superstitious. I can't help it. Then my mother-in-law persuaded me to call him Robert after his grandfather. Everyone calls him Bob. I don't care for that, really, but finally I've fallen in step. . . . I can never understand why he's always in such a foul temper with me. At bottom, I don't believe he's a particularly difficult child. Just hates the sight of me! I suppose that's what it is. I'm quite certain if I was to try to give him the rest of his dinner, he'd be screaming his head off in no time."

"Perhaps it's because your own nerves are on edge."

"Do you think he's aware of it?"

"I'm sure of it."

As soon as he'd finished feeding, Bob fell asleep at once.

"We'd better have our meal now. Come along, Alice."

Without expecting any result, Jeanne nevertheless went and called Louise, speaking through the locked door.

"Lunch is ready, Louise. Would you like to come down? Or would you rather I brought something up to you?"

No answer. So Jeanne and Alice sat down alone together in the dining room, where three places had been laid. To Alice's surprise, it was a proper meal, but it didn't occur to her afterward to clear away the things or help with the washing up. With the air of wandering aimlessly about, she had crossed the yard and gone into the office. It was only later that Jeanne realized it was to telephone without being overheard.

After that she went up to her room, still looking as though she had no object in view. The baby was sleeping very soundly. Then the leaves began to rustle, the doors to slam, so that Jeanne hardly heard the three little toots of the taxi's horn. The next thing she knew, the front door had opened and shut and the taxi had driven off. Alice had gone.

Jeanne calmly finished the dish washing. Then, realizing a thunderstorm was coming, she went around the house shutting the windows. She went into the blue room, where her brother was now laid out.

Although the room hadn't yet been transformed into a mortuary chapel, the undertakers had done their work well, and it already had the peaceful majesty of a lying in state. The blinds had been pulled down and the filtered light was soft and yellow. A white cloth around Robert's head kept the jaw from falling. It partly hid his face, but what was visible had already lost the horrible expression—a sort of ghastly sneer—that had been on it when they found him. They had put a clean white shirt on him, slightly starched, which contrasted with the waxy color of the flesh and the candles, which were already in place, though not yet lit.

Jeanne wasn't afraid of the dead. She drew a chair up to the bedside and sat down, with her hands in her lap, as though to have a chat with him. Her head was bent forward slightly and now and again her lips moved as though she really was talking to him.

Poor boy! And to have grown so fat! For he was even fatter and flabbier than she had thought. He must have suffered, since he had always been sensitive about it. At school he had been nicknamed Bubble Gum, and although he laughed and pretended not to mind, she had seen him crying about it when he thought nobody was looking. He had been pink at that time, blandly and blatantly pink, with innocent, candid eyes.

He was the Benjamin, never taken very seriously. He had had two brothers, Maurice and Gaston, but they had both been killed within a few days of each other during the first month of the 1914 war.

Robert, who was then in secondary school, wanted desperately to join up, and he was deeply mortified—much more so than anybody realized—when, two years later, he had gone before a medical board and been turned down.

"They wouldn't even tell me why," he protested indignantly, while his father merely shrugged his shoulders.

Poor boy! Yes, poor fat boy! He trembled and stuttered in

36

front of his father and was shy with girls. Perhaps because his father was a hard drinker, he reached the age of twenty without ever having touched a glass of spirits, and only smoked his first cigarette—for the sake of being like the others—when he went to the university, where he spent two years.

Jeanne wondered what circumstances had thrown him and Louise together, what he had been like as a young man in love, and how he had gone about proposing. She was already gone then, and corresponded only rarely with her family. She had heard only of the marriage and of the birth of the first boy, Julien, the one who had been killed in the car crash.

The big house was silent and empty around them. Behind her locked door, Louise had probably fallen into a heavy sleep.

Jeanne had to get up from her chair by Robert's side when she heard the baby wake up.

"Well, my little man? You're going to be as good as gold with your old Aunt Jeanne, aren't you?"

Bob appeared to understand. He looked at her gravely. He wasn't in the least afraid of her, or surprised that a new person had come to look after him. He let her pick him up, and, while she changed him, had a good look around. Reassured, he looked once again at Jeanne, first frowning, then bursting into a smile.

"You see, it's all quiet in the house now. Presently Aunt Jeanne'll give you your food and put you back to bed again."

It was on leaving the blue room and going into Alice's, where the shutters were not closed, that she noticed the heavy dark clouds. The street was in a sort of false twilight, in which the girls' summer dresses and the white houses looked crudely livid.

At four o'clock the lightning began to zip through a range of black clouds that seemed to be hanging motionless over the station, but, oddly enough, no thunder followed, nor did it rain, and the air was still heavy and sticky.

"Just the same, your Aunt Jeanne will have to go back to the hotel to get her things."

She was on the point of doing so then and there, and almost picked up the baby to take him with her. But an obscure feeling prevented her from leaving the house, so there was nothing for it but to stay as she was, in clothes that were drenched with perspiration and the shoes that pinched her feet.

It was at half past four that the telephone rang. Jeanne didn't answer it at once, to give Louise a chance to take the call herself in her bedroom. But the telephone went on ringing, becoming shriller and shriller, and Bob began to whimper. So she picked him up, went down to the dining room, and lifted the receiver.

"Hello! Is that you, Alice? . . . It's Henri. Is Father in?"

She was on the point of telling him who she was, but he rattled on so breathlessly that she hardly got a chance to put a word in. Behind his voice were strange noises like machinery.

"What sort of a mood is he in? Is Mother with him? It's most important that I know. Where is he? What's he doing? What did he say when he found I'd taken the car?"

"Alice has gone out," she managed to say at last.

A silence. The boy at the other end of the line was obviously taken aback.

"Who's speaking?" he asked suspiciously.

"Aunt Jeanne. Your father's sister."

"What? The one who lives in South America? You've come home? . . . Can I speak to my father?"

"I'm afraid you can't."

"I must. It's most important. Has he gone out?"

"No."

"Then what's the matter? Why can't you get him?"

"He can't come to the telephone."

"Do you mean he's ill? Because I went off with the car?"

"No."

A moment's hesitation.

"Is Mother up to her tricks again?"

38

"Your father's dead, Henri."

Another silence, a longer, oppressive, silence; then in a toneless voice the boy said to someone standing by him:

"My father's dead."

"Look . . . Are you there?"

"Yes. Where's Mother?"

"Your mother's in bed."

He muttered between his teeth.

"I understand."

"Where are you telephoning from? And why did you want to speak to your father?"

She had the impression he was crying, not so much from grief perhaps as from the feeling that his world was collapsing around him.

"I'm a long way away. I don't know what to do. I can't get home."

"Where are you?"

"In a little village in the Calvados. I'm more than three hundred kilometers from home. We've had a breakdown. A serious one. The back axle. The people in the garage here have been working on it for the last hour. I've been trying for ages to get through to you. I don't know what's wrong with the line. The thing is the car's practically ready now, only they won't let it go unless I pay the bill, and I've run out of money. I thought if Father spoke to the man here . . ."

"Ask him to come to the phone."

She promised the proprietor of the garage that he'd be paid. Then it was the boy again, saying:

"Thanks so much, Aunt Jeanne."

"Are you alone?"

He hesitated a moment.

"No."

"With friends?"

"With a friend, yes, and we've a couple of girls with us. I may as well tell you right out, since you're bound to find out sooner or later."

"Promise me you'll drive carefully."

"I promise."

"I'll wait up till you come. All night if necessary. There's no hurry."

"Thanks."

They were silent again. And then, because neither had anything more to say, they each hung up.

"And now if I haven't got to change you again, you little piddler!"

Once again the stairs, which were higher and steeper than she had remembered them. When she came back, she put the baby down on the kitchen floor, and while she got his next meal ready, he crawled about and played happily with his feet. She had time to feed him, clean him, and put him back to bed before the storm broke at last, and the first cracks of thunder found her nibbling a bit of cheese in the kitchen. The day had turned so dark that she had had to switch the light on, while the rest of the house was steeped in murky gloom.

The rain came down in torrents, splashing on the metal roof of the office, on the windowsills, and on the flagstones of the courtyard, which at once became black and shiny. The rainwater pipes gurgled, gutters overflowed. Flashes of lightning followed each other in quick succession, and from the claps of thunder you would have thought the sky was being rent asunder.

No doubt it was because all other noises were drowned by the thunder that she didn't hear Louise come down. Turning around, she started at the sight of her standing in the doorway, her face pale, rings under her shining eyes, having groped her way down the dark staircase, not daring to touch an electric switch on account of the lightning.

Louise didn't know what to say or what to do with herself. She looked more like an intruder than a woman in her own house. She was no longer wearing the black dress she had had on that morning, but had slipped on a dark purple robe, which she clutched around her as though she felt cold.

Jeanne felt slightly ashamed at being found like that, sitting at the kitchen table, eating, and she got up quickly as though she was at fault.

"Sit down," said Louise, drawing one of the white-painted chairs up to the table and sitting down herself.

"Henri called."

"I know."

"Were you listening?"

"Yes."

"I wasn't sure what I ought to say. Finally I thought I'd better tell him."

"You were quite right. There was no point in keeping it from him."

"Wouldn't you like something to eat?"

"I'm not hungry."

"But you've had nothing since breakfast."

"It doesn't matter. I'm not hungry."

She started at a clap of thunder louder than ever, and her lips moved as though she was muttering a prayer.

"Jeanne!"

"Yes."

"I'm afraid."

"What of?"

"Of the storm. Of the thought of dying . . . Has Alice gone?"

"Yes."

"I knew she would. I knew she wouldn't spend a night here, with Robert's body in the house. What's more, I knew she'd leave Bob behind. . . . I'm afraid, Jeanne."

"There's nothing to be frightened of."

"Listen! It's right overhead."

It was indeed. In fact, the next flash caught a tree in a neighboring garden. The crack was terrific. With her nerves on edge, Louise was no longer able to keep still, and she sprang to her feet and started pacing feverishly up and down the room.

After a furtive glance at Jeanne, who was still sitting at the table, she blurted out:

"You despise me, don't you?"

"No, Louise. I don't."

"Then you pity me, which comes to the same thing."

41

"You don't need anybody's pity."

"That's what you say, but you think just the opposite. I'm afraid, Jeanne. Why did Robert do that? Don't tell me it's my own fault. It's not true. I swear it isn't. I want you to believe me, Jeanne. I must have someone to believe me.

"This morning I was out of my mind. I don't remember a word of what I said to you, but I know it was nasty. I wanted to hurt you. I had to hurt someone; I was suffering so much myself. You don't believe me, do you?"

"Yes. I believe you."

"Are you sure all the windows are shut?"

"I've been around the house."

"At the top too?"

"Everywhere."

"What about him?"

"Everything's been done. They've laid him out in the blue room."

"I know. I heard them."

"Wouldn't you like to come and see him with me?"

"Anything but that," cried Louise. "I simply couldn't. I haven't the strength. Can't you understand that? I'm afraid! I'm afraid! That's all I can tell you, over and over again, I'm scared, scared to death. And you can't understand. . . ."

"Sit down. Try to relax."

"I can't. I can't keep still. It hurts too much. My whole body aches, and my head. . . ."

"I'll make you some coffee."

"You're kind."

And, as Jeanne put some water on to boil, she muttered pensively:

"Why are you doing all this? Why did you come? And at just this moment! It's as though you knew how things were with us and wanted . . ."

Her face changed, her features contracted, and her eyes narrowed with the same inquisitive look they had had as a young girl.

"Had you by chance heard something?"

"No. I came because I . . ."

But Louise wasn't listening, following her own train of thought. In any case Jeanne would have been hard put to finish her sentence.

"Did you get a letter from somebody?"

"No."

"Did Robert ever complain to you about me?"

"I haven't heard from him for twenty years. He didn't even know where I was."

It was strange. Louise's voice seemed to undergo a change with each phase of the thunderstorm. Whenever the thunder and lightning came closer, she became humble, supplicating, pitiful, and each time they receded, allowing her to hope the storm was over, she would rally, her voice becoming quieter and firmer. Then she would bend her head down and shoot little glances at Jeanne from under her eyebrows.

"At any rate, you knew Father was dead, didn't you?"

"Quite by chance, I stumbled on the notice in a French paper."

"What? In South America?"

That was a trap. Jeanne couldn't fail to see it. It was too obvious.

"No. In Cairo."

"So it's true you lived in Cairo?"

"Yes. Why?"

"Oh. Nothing."

Hadn't she said that morning she'd met somebody who'd spoken of Jeanne? She knew more than she wanted to admit.

"You mean the notice put in by the notary?"

When she had been in Egypt, Jeanne hardly ever read a newspaper except such French ones as happened to fall into her hands. Then, because it was a rare treat, she read every word from the first page to the last. It was thus that she had come upon the notice in the personal column of a Paris paper.

Information concerning the whereabouts of Jeanne Marie Hortense Martineau, born at Pont Saint-Jean June 5th, 1894, is desired by Maître Bigeois, notary, Pont Saint-Jean, who is winding up the estate of her father. Please communicate as quickly as possible, either direct or through consular authorities.

"Why didn't you show up?"
It was in a listless voice that Jeanne answered:
"I really don't know."
"You realized what it meant, of course?"
"Yes. But it was too late to come for the funeral. The paper was already two months old."
"Didn't you need the money?"
"What's the point of going into all that?"
"Forgive me for what I said this morning. I knew it wasn't true, that it wasn't for that reason that you came."
"Thanks. Two lumps?"
"Only one. And no milk, please."
"Sure you wouldn't like me to make you a sandwich? There's a nice bit of cold beef."
"No, really. I'm not hungry. . . . It's coming back again, Jeanne."
And, as Jeanne went toward the door to listen for any sound from the baby:
"Stay here. Don't leave me alone. Did I hurt you dreadfully this morning?"
"No."
"What did Dr. Bernard say about me?"
"Nothing."
"He didn't insist on seeing me?"
"He wanted you to come down but, since you didn't, he suggested the inspector leave you in peace."
"And Alice?"
She lumbered on, her mind set on one idea. Sometimes the thunder and lightning made her lose the thread, but she always picked it up again.
"What did Alice tell you?"
"That in her state of nerves she wasn't fit to have a child and that Bob had an aversion to her."

44

"But about me? I'm quite sure she talked about me."

Jeanne knew very well what she was driving at. But how was she to tell her that she had understood without anybody's help, that she hadn't been particularly surprised, and that she herself had given way, first at the station at Poitiers and later in the dining room of the Anneau d'Or?

Before she could make up her mind, Louise was off again, saying emphatically:

"I'm a bad woman, Jeanne."

Did she mean it? Yes, it was at least to some extent sincere.

"Go on! Nobody's altogether either good or bad."

"I don't see why they shouldn't be. I've tried to be good, altogether good. I've tried all my life. Nobody believes it. Nobody's ever believed it. They all hate me. Even Robert. It's years since he looked at me as he did at first, and I could see he'd lost all hope. There's been a wall between us. A glass wall. We could see each other, but could make no real contact.

"It hasn't been easy for me here. If I cried for any reason, if I was upset or discouraged, his father used to shrug his shoulders, point to the door, and say icily:

"'If you're going to be hysterical you can go to your room.'

"He thought I was doing it on purpose to attract attention. It wasn't true. I've never tried to play on people's feelings."

Another clap of thunder, and she gripped Jeanne's arm, pleading piteously:

"Now you've come, you mustn't leave us, Jeanne. You mustn't despise me. You mustn't think I'm altogether bad. When I first came to this house, I was young and innocent and full of good will. I wanted everybody to be happy. I thought I could make them happy. But do you know what my father-in-law called me, right from the start?

"'That Taillefer girl.'

"And you know how he spoke—with every word cutting like a knife.

"Even Baba—she was the maid they had then—even Baba

despised me. If I tried to help with the housework she'd snatch my duster out of my hands.

" 'You can leave that to me.'

"As if I was completely useless. As if I was a mere visitor in the house.

"Do you hear, Jeanne? It's coming back again. It's simply going round and round over the town. They're always like that. Old Bernard used to say it was the river that attracted them. . . . What was I saying? I can't remember. . . . But I'm boring you."

"Drink up your coffee."

"All right. But it's too hot. . . . Even my children . . . You'll see how they treat me. . . . As for Alice, she's got only one wish: to get away from this house as soon as she can. She'll abandon her child if necessary. I wonder if she'll come back after the funeral. Do you think she will?"

"I'm sure of it."

"I'm not. Far from it. Six weeks after Bob was born, I found her one evening . . ."

A flash of lightning lit up the whole house. This time it really did seem they were in for it. Louise fell on her knees and with both hands clutched at her sister-in-law's dress.

"You see! We'll all be killed. . . ."

Jeanne was standing now. All she could think of doing was to pat Louise's head, which she did absent-mindedly.

"I think I can hear Bob," she said after a moment.

"You needn't worry about him. He's not afraid. He's too young to know. . . . I'm sorry, but . . ."

"Hush!"

"What is it?"

As Jeanne moved, Louise still clung to her skirt, dragging herself along on her knees.

"Nothing. A shutter banging. I thought it was the child."

She realized Louise was jealous of the concern she showed for the baby, and might at any moment break into a fit of rage.

"Get up now and drink your coffee. If the lightning does strike us . . ."

"Shut up! For heaven's sake."

"Then calm down. Soon Henri will be coming back. And no doubt his sister'll be coming back this evening too. You'll have to tell her what's happened."

"They don't give a hang for me, any more than they did for their father. Less. They did now and again show some consideration for him."

"You're in a black mood, Louise."

"What do you mean by that?"

"Nothing. Or . . . just what I say. You wallow in your misery. Instead of looking at things fairly and squarely."

"Is that all you meant? Really? I know Alice has been talking. You may as well admit it."

"She didn't say a word about it. Nor did Dr. Bernard. I simply smelled your breath when you opened your door this morning. I understood at once."

"And you're not disgusted with me?"

"No."

"Why?"

"Because I know a thing or two."

"Don't you think it's my own fault?"

"No."

"Don't you think I'm a good-for-nothing?"

"Weak, perhaps. That's all."

"I've tried my utmost. I've gone for days, for weeks even, without touching the stuff, taking precautions that there be no bottles lying about, and avoiding going into the warehouse. But I could never keep it up. It's no use, Jeanne. I can't keep off it. I'm a worthless creature, no use to anyone. I'm the one who ought to be dead. . . ."

"Don't say such things."

"I must. I must get it off my chest. Ever since this morning, I've been haunted by one thought. I didn't sleep a wink. I heard every sound in the house. I followed all your movements. And all the time the same question was nagging at me. . . .

"Tell me frankly, Jeanne. . . . It's years and years since you saw him, but he's your brother, nonetheless. . . . Tell me:

47

was it my doing? Was it on account of me that he did it?

"Tell me. I must know. If I've got to go on with that question gnawing away at me! No! It would be too awful. . . . If it was my fault, someone must forgive me."

"That's all right."

"Can you forgive me?"

"I've nothing to forgive."

"Can't you forgive me in your brother's name?"

"I don't think he had anything against you. I'm sure of it. And the proof is that, when he went, it was he who asked your forgiveness."

Louise was thoughtful. She murmured:

"That's true."

But a ray of hope could only light up her mind for a moment. Then she was floundering again worse than ever, assailed by thoughts, some black, some gray, from which she groped desperately for an escape.

"You see, Robert was a good man. I'm bad. I've tried, God knows. But I couldn't stick it out. I never shall be able to. You mustn't leave me, Jeanne. Ever. I couldn't bear to stay here alone. I'm afraid of the way the children will look at me when they get back. You saw how Alice was this morning. Not one comforting word for me. They're all like that and always have been.

"Except Robert. Earlier, that is. Then he got tired of it and threw in the sponge. I suppose he hoped for something, then saw it was no use and gave it up as hopeless. He became more and more shut up in himself, year by year. He could still laugh and joke at times, but only in the presence of visitors or if he thought he was alone with the children. Sometimes he'd hum a tune while dressing, but not if I was there. If I came into the room, he'd stop at once and a vague, distant look would spread over his face."

"You make mountains out of molehills."

"I could tell you almost to a day when it started. Immediately after his father's death, or practically. That's ten years ago, and the children were quite young. The business was prosperous, and we were making lots of money. It was then we set about modernizing the house. . . . Jeanne! . . . That's the bridge!"

No. The bridge was still intact. The lightning was probably a good deal farther off than it seemed. The rumbling thunder died away, and once again there was nothing to be heard but the steady patter of the rain. The two women remained in the brightly lit white kitchen, while all the rest of the house was dark. It didn't occur to either of them to go and sit elsewhere.

"If I'm going to sleep here I'll have to let them know at the Anneau d'Or. I'd better call them up."

"Not during the storm. On no account. It's much too dangerous."

"I could nip around there as soon as it's over and get my things."

She unhooked the apron, which had already become *her* apron, and tied the strings behind her back.

"What are you going to do?"

"Get the supper ready."

"Who for?"

"For you and me, and for the children if they turn up."

"Suppose they come back late?"

Jeanne didn't answer and got to work. Louise stood leaning on the sink, obviously feeling useless as she watched her sister-in-law going to and fro.

"I don't know how you manage it."

"Manage what?"

But what was the good of explaining? She knew very well what Louise meant, though she would have been at a loss to find an answer. And what a long answer it would have been!

"Have some more coffee."

"No. Thanks all the same. You're very kind to me."

"There's just one thing I haven't been able to find. That's the trash pail. It used to be just outside the pantry door, on the left."

Louise took a couple of steps and opened a sort of enameled drawer, which provided a chute for the trash.

"Can't I help you?" she asked, not very convincingly.

49

"No. You sit down. The storm's nearly over."

"Do you think so?"

"It won't be long now. By the way, I promised to call the undertaker this evening about the notices. He wants the list as soon as possible. Of your friends, that is. The business people he'll get from the chief clerk in the morning. . . . He's going to see the priest about giving absolution."

Louise didn't take it in at once. At such moments, her pupils contracted, as they did when she was suspicious of anything. Like a cat's. Till they were nothing but two bright black dots.

"Ah! I see! I hadn't thought about that."

Almost imperceptibly the storm moved away and the rain shrank to a few drips, till presently the house and kitchen were wrapped in the silence of night.

From time to time Jeanne went and listened in the doorway for any sound from the baby upstairs.

4

The funeral was on Wednesday and, thus far, Louise had had no relapse. She gave the impression of being on her best behavior, as though she had made a resolution, and Jeanne noticed that every bottle had been hidden out of sight, even the one of cooking sherry.

When the children had arrived home on Sunday evening, within barely half an hour of each other, Louise was washed out and incapable of rising to the occasion. She had simply sat passively in a corner, leaving Jeanne to bear the brunt.

It was Henri who arrived first. He had a key and burst in without warning at ten o'clock, leaving the car in front of the door. The rain had long since stopped and the moon had just come out. He was disconcerted at first to find the whole house in darkness, except the kitchen, where Jeanne and Louise were still sitting. He wore no hat. His hair was fair and thick, and he had his father's pale-blue eyes. He was, however, much shorter than his father, though broad-shouldered and firm of bearing.

In the doorway he frowned, dazzled by the bright light, and perhaps unconsciously displeased to find everything in the house changed, his mother sitting at a corner of the kitchen table where normally it would have been the maid, and near her a fat, pasty-faced woman who studied him with calm curiosity.

It was in an aggressive, almost accusing tone that he flung out:

"How did it happen?"

Unthinkingly he had addressed his aunt. Aware of it suddenly, he turned toward his mother.

"Were you with him?"

Louise seemed to shrink, as though she felt herself guilty, and Jeanne realized she was much too scared to answer. So she answered for her:

"Your mother was at church."

"Was nobody in?"

"Only Alice, who was busy with the baby."

"Was it a heart attack?"

He breathed heavily, standing with his feet slightly apart, and, if he spoke unnecessarily loudly, it was doubtless because he was on the verge of breaking down.

"Look here, Henri, you'd better be treated as a man and told the truth at once. Keep calm. Don't lose your head. Your father hanged himself."

He had come in flushed with emotion and from the drive through the night air. From one second to the next, without the least transition, his face turned white. He stood absolutely still. Only his Adam's apple jerked.

They hadn't noticed Jeanne get to her feet. She stood by the boy, putting a hand on his shoulder.

"Come, now! You're going to be a man, aren't you, Henri?"

For a moment he made no protest. Then, almost angrily, he pushed her hand away and dived out of the room into the hall, where he threw himself full length on the stairs, buried his head in his arms, and broke into loud sobs.

52

His mother, huddled on her chair, was wringing her hands till the fingers were white at the knuckles. She opened her mouth, and Jeanne, seeing she was going to scream, snapped at her almost brutally:

"Shut up! None of that! If you can't bottle it up, you'd better go back to your room."

Louise submitted meekly, and they stayed in the kitchen, listening to the boy's sobs, sometimes raucous, sometimes muffled, like a child's. Sometimes, like the baby upstairs, he would stop altogether, only to break out louder than ever. Louise couldn't take her eyes off Jeanne, and she watched her intently as the latter got up after a moment to put the soup on.

That done, she went out, turned on the light, and spoke to the boy in her quiet, elderly voice:

"Come up to see him now. He's upstairs in your sister's room. Only be quiet, so as not to wake Bob."

The lights were switched on one after the other, while Louise sat trembling in the kitchen, feeling neglected. The voices from upstairs were now no more than a murmur.

"Don't be afraid, Henri. He wasn't angry with you. He wasn't angry with anyone. His last act was to ask you all to forgive him."

The boy, still deathly pale, clutched the doorjamb, unable to go in.

"Kiss him."

She led him up to the bed and gently pushed him forward, keeping one hand on his shoulder. He bent down and lightly kissed his father's forehead. Then he stiffened.

"That's all. Now come away."

On the landing he stopped.

"I don't want to come down."

"Come on. We can't talk here."

He gave in and walked downstairs in front of her. At the kitchen door he hesitated, then went in, avoiding his mother's eyes.

"I don't suppose you've had any supper."

53

"I won't eat anything."

"You'd better have a plate of soup, at any rate. We'll be needing your help tomorrow. In fact, we need it now."

It was his mother's presence that seemed to embarrass him, and it was on her account that he didn't want to soften. Sulkily, he repeated:

"No. I won't eat anything."

Jeanne took no notice of that and helped him to some soup. It was only then that he began to look with curiosity at this new relation he found installed in the house, who behaved and talked to him as though she'd always lived there. What struck him more than anything was the attitude of his mother, quietly taking a back seat, miraculously calm. He had expected to find her completely out of control.

"Now eat it up."

He demurred for a second, not yet prepared to give in, then bent his head over his plate.

He was still at it, absent-mindedly, when his sister, who had no key, knocked lightly on the door. At the same time a car could be heard driving off.

"That's Mad," he said, springing to his feet. "I'll go."

And he dashed out of the room. Jeanne didn't attempt to stop him. For quite a while the brother and sister were talking in an undertone, with long silences, just inside the front door. Then a white figure, with two long bare legs, quickly crossed the hall and ran up the stairs.

Henri came back to the kitchen and, sitting down again in his place, remarked:

"She knew."

Louise was on the point of asking a question, but a look from her sister-in-law stopped her, and it was Henri who volunteered the information himself. He was feeling the need to talk.

"They were stopped by a policeman for driving too fast. Just on the outskirts of town. He asked for their papers. Recognizing Mad, he was astonished to see her driving about like that when her father was dead."

"Is she coming down?"

"I think so. She's gone up to change."

"But . . ."

Jeanne had suddenly remembered it was in the girl's room that they'd put Robert. Henri understood.

"I told her. It didn't stop her."

Presently he added:

"Isn't Alice here?"

"No. She's gone. But she'll be back for the funeral."

At that last word he nearly broke down again. He sniffed several times, but managed to control himself. Having finished his soup, he didn't know quite what to do.

"You'd better put the car away."

"Yes. I'd quite forgotten the car."

"You stay here," said Jeanne to Louise.

It was more than ten minutes since Madeleine had gone up. Once again Jeanne climbed the stairs. She saw the light was on in the blue room and gently pushed open the door.

The girl was now in a dark-blue dress, while her wet shorts and blouse were lying on the floor.

She was sitting on a chair by the farthest corner of the bed, huddled up, with her elbows on her knees and her chin in her hands, looking steadily at her father.

She wasn't crying. Nor did she move a muscle when her aunt came in. She took not the slightest notice of her till the latter, as she had with Henri, tried to put her hand on the girl's shoulder. Then with a rough movement Madeleine pushed her away, and for a moment Jeanne almost thought she was going to hit her.

"You must come down now."

Not a word. Not a look.

"You can't stay here, Madeleine. I'm your Aunt Jeanne. Your mother's downstairs. Henri's there too—at least he's just putting the car away."

"Haven't I the right to stay with my father?" hissed the girl.

"Not now, Mad. We want you downstairs."

She led the way out, and Mad followed, though obviously not in any submissive spirit. Out of defiance, rather. There was something haughty, even contemptuous, about her whole bearing.

In the kitchen, it wasn't to Jeanne that she spoke, but to her mother, yet her voice was no less harsh and disrespectful than it had been upstairs.

"Well? What do you want with me?"

"There's no need to speak to me like that, Mad."

Jeanne thought she'd better intervene.

"Look here, Madeleine, you'd better have something to eat. After that you can go to bed in Henri's room. He can go up to the floor above. Unless you'd rather go up there yourself."

Mad's lips quivered as she looked daggers at Jeanne. Henri was quite startled by the sight of her when he came back, smoking a cigarette he'd lit crossing the yard.

"What's the matter, Mad?" he asked.

"Nothing. Only, they said they wanted me, so I came down. Since it's not true . . ."

He made a movement to stop her, then thought better of it, and she stalked out of the room and went upstairs again.

Jeanne didn't get a chance to warn the hotel she wouldn't be sleeping there, still less to get her things. She merely took her dress off and got into Alice's bed in her slip. The crib was alongside her and for a long time she listened to the baby's breathing before finally falling asleep.

It was Bob who woke her up, at about six. A pale convalescent sun was reflected by the slats of the shutters. In order not to wake up the others, she took him with her when she hurried down to the kitchen to get his food ready. Having fed him, she made some coffee for herself, and at seven o'clock, still taking him with her, she crossed the bridge and went into the Anneau d'Or.

The proprietors, who had as usual been working late on Sunday, were not yet down. In the café, where the chairs were piled on the tables, Raphäel, unshaved, was sweeping up the sawdust that covered the floor.

"Is Désirée around?" she asked.

"I suppose she's having her breakfast, since it won't be long now before the guests start ringing for theirs. Particularly on a Monday, when there are always some going off early."

"Would you mind telling her Jeanne would like a word with her?"

There were mirrors all around the walls over the settees, and she saw herself standing there with the astonished baby in her arms. It didn't even make her smile, and, if her face expressed anything at all, it was a sort of quiet resignation.

"Jeanne!" cried Désirée, surprised to find her there, and still more to find her with a baby.

"He's my great-nephew, Julien's boy," she explained. "There was nobody I could give him to, so I brought him along. The others are still asleep. . . ."

"I heard about what happened yesterday. Poor Jeanne! How terrible for you! And to think you were here the night before!"

Jeanne realized she was probably wrong to do what she was about to do, and that sooner or later it might have awkward repercussions, perhaps create animosities, but her mind was made up and she was in a hurry.

"Look here, Désirée, I wonder if you'd do me a great favor. Could you come and help at my sister-in-law's, even if it's for a few days? I'd help you all I could, but I simply can't cope with the whole house single-handed."

"Of course not. I understand. But . . ."

She hesitated. For a few minutes the two women discussed the matter in an undertone, while Raphäel went on sweeping around them. Finally Désirée went off toward the kitchen to find her mistress, who had no doubt come down by this time. It was a quarter of an hour before she returned. From the doorway she made a little sign, which told her friend at once that all was arranged, for it was one of the secret signs they had used in the convent.

"It was a bit of a tussle, but in the end the Mother Superior gave her consent. As a matter of fact, they don't like me any too much here and aren't sorry to be seeing the last of me, particularly since I was able to persuade another girl to take my place, one who had come in only for the weekend. I'll have to help with the breakfasts, but I ought to be with you before ten. In the meantime Raphäel will carry your suitcase over. I told them you'd look in again to pay the bill. Now that they know who you are . . ."

Louise came down at half past eight looking paler and more washed out than ever.

"Have you seen anything of the children?"

"Not yet. I guess they're still asleep."

"Did you go out? I thought I heard the door."

"Yes. I went to the hotel. And I asked Désirée—you remember Désirée, who was at the convent with us—I asked her to come and lend a hand here, if only for a few days. She's working at the hotel now. They've given her leave to come at once."

"Do you mean she agreed? It's ages since anyone here has consented to work for us."

She didn't seem to mind Jeanne's having taken the initiative. She took whatever came. She accepted everything that Jeanne proposed or decided, only too glad to lean on her.

"I don't even know where Mad slept."

"For a long time she was leaning out one of the third-floor windows. I was asleep before she went to bed."

"And Henri?"

"I think he slept all right. Before turning in, he tried to talk to his sister, but she sent him away."

The police inspector called, and then the undertaker, just as the local paper's one and only reporter knocked on the door. Fortunately, Désirée had just arrived. Jeanne handed her the baby, whom so far she had been carrying all morning.

"I will be busy for the next half hour or so. Try to get him to sleep. But it probably won't be easy."

In spite of the sunshine, a grizzly atmosphere seemed to pervade the house. Everybody felt flat and empty, as after

58

hours of weeping, though, as a matter of fact, few tears had been shed. Even Louise, contrary to all expectations, managed to meet the situation with a relatively brave face. And sometimes, when she looked at her sister-in-law, she was able to produce a wan, forced smile.

She wanted to be nice to everybody. She had always wanted to be nice. Perhaps she realized how precarious was the calm that had settled on the house, a calm that a single misplaced word or tactless action might suffice to shatter.

She moved about cautiously, watching her step, calculating every movement, as people do in a sickroom.

Jeanne didn't see the two children come down. A man she didn't know had come into the house, by the back door, and asked to see Louise. He was about thirty years old, and at once she guessed he was the chief clerk.

He had been talking for some time with Louise in one of the living rooms, when the latter called out:

"Jeanne! Are you busy? Could you spare us a moment?"

In another room the undertaker stood stiffly, with his hat in his hand, waiting for the promised list.

"This is Monsieur Sallenave, Jeanne, our chief clerk, who for a long time has been Robert's right-hand man. He's come with bad news, and I don't know what to do. Perhaps you could suggest something. I'm absolutely out of my depth in these matters. I'm sorry to leave it all to you, Jeanne, but would you mind having a talk with him?"

And, turning to the clerk:

"You might take my sister-in-law into the office, Monsieur Sallenave. You can tell her everything, since she's one of the family. She's got a much better head than I have and may be able to suggest a way out."

As they left, Jeanne turned around to say:

"Don't forget the list, Louise."

"I'll get to it right away."

"Go ahead, Monsieur Sallenave, though, in spite of what my sister-in-law said, my brother's business is no concern of mine."

Unlike the house, the business premises had remained unchanged throughout the years. The same glass-paneled partition was there, separating Robert's office from what had always been the chief clerk's, and, better still, the same stove that Jeanne had known as a child and on which she had many a time roasted chestnuts when her grandfather was away on some business trip. From the hooks under a shelf of dark wood hung the same chased silver cups that were filled with wine for customers to taste.

"I suppose things are in a bad way. I may as well ask you at once: do you think my brother committed suicide for financial reasons?"

Sallenave was a simple and straightforward man of humble origin, who had risen by dint of hard work. He no doubt had firm convictions and somewhat cast-iron ideas, and some words shocked him. At the word "suicide" he bridled slightly, and Jeanne regretted having spoken so bluntly.

"Undoubtedly Monsieur Martineau's financial position has been thoroughly undermined. For the last two years or so he had had a job to meet his obligations—like many others, for that matter. He was certainly aware that some were due to be met today, but, since you ask my opinion, I don't think that's sufficient reason to explain what's happened."

"There are several things that I'd like to know, Monsieur Sallenave, and perhaps it would be best for me to ask my questions. I know little enough about business and nothing whatever about my brother's affairs, and I want to get some sort of idea of the situation."

"Ask me anything you like."

"It's over thirty-five years since I left home. At that period the business was flourishing, and I imagine it still was long after that. When did the tide begin to turn?"

"That's not very easy to answer, because it didn't happen all at once. I came here as a junior clerk just before the war, a few months before your father died, and at that time business was tolerably good—I would't put it higher. We got along, as they say. Then war broke out, and, as you probably know, the price of wine soared, rising from day to day."

He was picking his words, wanting to be absolutely frank and objective, though he was embarrassed at being obliged to broach certain subjects.

"Monsieur Robert made a lot of money," he said solemnly.

"On the black market?"

This time she was purposely blunt. She didn't want him to spend hours beating about the bush.

"Not exactly. It depends on how you look at it. For a time, admittedly, certain things were done that were not quite in order. The regulations were so onerous that we might as well have shut up shop altogether as try to carry them out. To get around them, the books had to be kept in a manner that in normal times would have been most reprehensible."

"I see. And it was during the war that the house was modernized, wasn't it?"

"It badly needed repairs. Monsieur Louis would never allow it to be touched, let alone modernized. Wine was in such demand that, if you had some to offer, you could get anything you liked. Building materials, for instance. Even the most unprocurable."

"What happened then?"

"Were you in France at the time of the Liberation?"

"No."

"For several days, weeks even, it looked as though Monsieur Robert was going to be in trouble. Like many others, he received threatening letters. A committee was set up, and there was talk of sending him to a concentration camp, but it wasn't long before things quieted down."

"But it was damaging to the business, I suppose."

"No. I can't say it was. In fact, business went very well indeed. It was another two years before matters came to a head—during an election campaign."

"Did my brother go in for politics?"

"Not exactly. But he was very open-handed, and he thought he was called on, on account of his position here, to

61

subscribe liberally to any cause that came along. Even political parties. All of them. He couldn't refuse anybody. He gave them quite a lot. More than was wise, and I wouldn't be surprised if it wasn't that which got him into trouble. Whether it was generosity or prudence—like taking out an insurance policy—he gave money to the Communists too. It did him no good. A witch hunt was started. As a matter of fact, it was really aimed at others, but he was roped in too. One day, when we least expected it, we received a note from the tax collector asking for further information about an income-tax return made four years previously.

"Monsieur Robert went around at once to see about it. He was on the best of terms with the mayor and other influential people, and for a time it looked as though everything was going to be smoothed out.

"The affair dragged on, and, if you ask me it was that long period of worry and uncertainty that got him down. He looked well. He was always on the go and full of confidence. Outwardly. Beneath the surface, he was no longer the same.

"And then . . . Do you remember Monsieur Bourgeois?"

"Gaston Bourgeois?"

Yes, she remembered a weedy, studious boy of thirteen, always up to his eyes in books. At that time he was already a friend of Robert's.

"He teaches philosophy at the secondary school. He was a close friend of your brother's, perhaps the only really intimate friend he had. Then, after the war, Monsieur Bourgeois suddenly stopped seeing him, wouldn't even nod to him in the street. There were others who did the same for a time, then thought better of it. Some of them apologized. But with Monsieur Bourgeois it was never patched up. . . . It goes against the grain to rake up all this, but you said you wanted to understand."

"Quite right, Monsieur Sallenave. So it comes to this—my brother had something on his conscience."

"That's putting it too strongly, though there were certainly things he was not quite happy about. . . . And then, when at last it looked as though everything was patched up here, the trouble started all over again, at the instigation of higher levels in Poitiers and Paris. Monsieur Robert made several trips and each time came back thinking he'd carried the day. Yet that didn't stop them sending an inspector here, who sat in my place for the best part of two months, going through all the books and papers with a fine-tooth comb. And all that time he never so much as opened his mouth except to ask a question.

"Meanwhile, Monsieur Robert rushed about, giving money away right and left, trying to pull strings. All to no purpose. The inspector won.

"It would take too long to explain the whole system of penalties. Suffice it that your brother was called upon to pay a sum that was absolutely ruinous. If he'd sold everything, including the house, he'd hardly have found the money.

"In the end, a compromise was reached and he didn't come out quite so badly. Since then the business has carried on; in fact, it's doing very well. But the trouble left it with a deficit which the profits are unable to overtake. At the end of every month we have to do a lot of juggling to tide us over to the next.

"You knew the house long before I did. The turnover to-day is probably twice what it was then, after allowing for the devaluation of the franc. And yet, Madame, this morning if you asked me for a mere thousand francs, I just wouldn't know where to find them. The big bills I can generally manage with a good deal of wangling. It's the ready cash for running expenses, for the little things that can't wait—that's the difficulty.

"It's been going on like this for the last two years, with a minor crisis once a month, sometimes twice.

"I can't very well go and explain things to the bank manager, who is already a bit cautious and inclined to hesitate before discounting our bills. I can't very well go and tell him that I absolutely must have ten thousand francs before twelve o'clock or the whole edifice will crash. If I can't pay certain bills this morning, it'll be all over town before the day's out, and people will go around saying that Monsieur Robert, as you suspected yourself, took his life because he was bankrupt."

"You've told my sister-in-law?"

"More or less. I didn't go into detail."

"What did she say?"

"That there was nothing she could do. That I'd better talk to you about it."

"Would ten thousand francs really see you through for the moment?"

"Hardly. I was quoting a figure more or less at random. Let me see . . ."

He took a bit of paper and jotted down some figures.

"Thirteen thousand five hundred would cover the more pressing claims."

"I'll bring you the money in a moment."

Her whole fortune was in her handbag and amounted to no more than eighteen thousand francs. Louise hadn't been far wrong: she had come to ask for money, not to give it.

It hadn't even occurred to her to demand her share of her father's estate. No, she had come humbly, as a beggar, old and worn out, tired of privations and no longer able to fend for herself.

"I'm most grateful to you," said M. Sallenave, beaming, as though she was doing him a personal service.

She smiled back at him.

There was quite a crowd assembled at the bridge. Some were sitting on the terrace of the Anneau d'Or, having a glass of white wine as they waited for the funeral procession to start.

After a lot of discussion, with people pulling different ways, the ecclesiastical authorities had finally decided there could be no absolution, only a benediction pronounced from the steps of Saint-Jean.

In the marketplace at least fifty carts stood unharnessed

with their shafts sticking up in the air, as on market days, having brought in farmers from the surrounding country, each of whom had gone in through the draped doorway to stand for a moment by the coffin, paying their respects to the dead.

In a dull black suit, Henri, whose cheeks had been flushed ever since he got up that morning, stood with lowered head near the candles, glancing furtively at all these people who came to shake him by the hand. Looking very small by his side was his mother, her face veiled, a handkerchief in the hollow of her hand. But she managed to mumble a few words of thanks to her visitors, the corners of her mouth drawn into a sad smile.

Alice was there with her parents. Her father was cashier in a bank in Poitiers. Not knowing what else to do with him, they had also brought along their twelve-year-old son.

It was only at the last minute that Mad had consented to take part in the proceedings. And it was no doubt her way of making her protest, when people came up to her to offer their condolences, that she stared them down blatantly, as though they were performing in some rather absurd pageant.

And without lowering her voice in the least, she would answer curtly:

"Thank you very much."

Or:

"You are too kind."

During the last three days she had never once offered to lend a hand. Right from Monday morning, when Jeanne, on her return from the office, had found her having her breakfast, she had made a point of treating her aunt in an offhand way, as though she were a servant. No, not quite that. For, if she wanted anything, she would invariably turn by choice to Désirée. Mostly she ignored Jeanne, merely accepting the fact that from now on, by some mysterious turn of events, there was an elderly woman with a face like a full moon wandering about the house.

She did it so ostentatiously that her brother was more than

once embarrassed and even indignant. In such moments he would make signs behind Jeanne's back, urging Mad to be a little more amenable.

If Jeanne addressed the girl, the latter would turn around with a surprised air, saying:

"I beg your pardon?"

Admittedly she did do anything that was expressly asked of her, but in such a lackadaisical way as to make it positively insulting.

At the funeral, everything went off satisfactorily for a while. It was only later that trouble broke out. It had been decided that the women should be present at the benediction, then return to the house, while the men proceeded slowly up to the cemetery. Jeanne didn't even go to the benediction. She had to stay behind to help Désirée, for, quite apart from having a meal to prepare for twenty people, who'd stay on for the rest of the day, there was also the baby to see to.

Jeanne was upstairs when Louise returned, accompanied by Mad, Alice, Alice's mother, an old Taillefer cousin, Mme Lallement, and two or three others.

As she went down, she passed Alice on the stairs, coming up on the pretext of having a look at Bob, who had with a bit of coaxing just gone off to sleep. The women were in the drawing room, which was pervaded by the smell of chrysanthemums. Mad was making no effort to play the hostess, but was sitting sulkily by the window with her hat in her lap.

There was an atmosphere of embarrassment in the room, and Jeanne noticed that Louise wasn't there. Going into the kitchen, she asked Désirée:

"Have you seen my sister-in-law?"

She looked for her for a minute or two, then gave up the search to attend to the visitors. Refreshments had already been set out on trays. The largest saucepans were simmering on the stove. In the dining room the table, with all its extra leaves in, was already laid, and there was even a box of cigars on the mantelpiece.

"Give me a hand, will you, Madeleine?"

The girl got up slowly, throwing her hat on her chair. Jeanne had already started pouring out the port. She pointed to the tray with the biscuits.

"If you wouldn't mind handing them around. Have you any idea where your mother is?"

Somehow the whole atmosphere was unreal. At the entrance, men on ladders were taking down the silver-fringed hangings. In every room hung a smell of half-faded flowers and burnings candles, to which another smell—that of the port—was soon to be added. Alice's mother talked in a monotonous voice, while the old Taillefer cousin kept nodding her head, holding her glass in front of her hairy chin.

It happened that both Mad and her aunt returned to the kitchen for refreshments. For a minute or two each was silently busy with what she had to do.

Suddenly Mad raised her head, then darted off toward the drawing room. Jeanne realized at once what was going on and followed. From the drawing room came the sound of Louise's voice. It wasn't her ordinary voice, at any rate not the one they had been hearing for the last few days. She was speaking now in the same vehement, tragic way as during the storm on Sunday night.

"All my life I've tried my utmost . . . All my life . . ."

Jeanne hurried as fast as she could, but was unable to overtake Mad. The voice went on:

"I know everyone despises me. . . ."

Reaching the doorway, Jeanne saw Mad, looking very straight and slim in her black dress, stride on her long legs across the room, ignoring the embarrassed visitors, stop dead in front of her mother, and give her a resounding slap.

"Go to your room," she snapped.

Louise raised her arm as though to ward off another blow and looked imploringly at her daughter.

"Don't hit me. Please don't hit me."

"Go to your room."

Mad was a whole head taller than her mother, whom she started pushing toward the door.

"You might at least let me tell them . . ."

"Get out."

And she followed as Louise hurried stumbling up the stairs. A moment later there was the sound of a door shutting, a key turning and being withdrawn.

Mad had locked her mother in.

5

It really looked as if the Fisolles, Alice's parents, were never going to leave, as if, knowing there were some spare rooms in the house, they were determined to miss their train.

In the course of the afternoon Jeanne had noticed Roger Fisolle, the father, talking to the chief clerk in the middle of the yard, and she had seen him, in a familiar, condescending manner, present the latter with a cigar, which he had certainly taken from the box in the dining room. She had attached no importance to it, however.

Most of the men, after a copious meal, had flushed cheeks and shining eyes and spoke almost as vociferously as at a marriage banquet. And as though they hadn't had enough to drink already, there were few who didn't wander off to inspect the cellars, reappearing later with the foreman, whose hand they would shake earnestly.

Jeanne lost sight of Fisolle for a while, but at six o'clock she saw him coming away from the office, looking worried and self-important.

As for Alice's mother, in the absence of the hostess, still locked in her room, it was she who had taken the lead in the conversation, talking at length about her daughter's studies, which had unfortunately been curtailed by her marriage.

"Afterward, it was too late."

By "afterward" she meant after Julien's death.

"It's a terrible thing to be thrown back on one's own resources at the age of barely twenty, with a child on one's hands."

Luckily the boy, who had all along been insufferable, disappeared late in the afternoon, having demanded some money from his mother with which to buy ice cream. Alice never once proposed to help with the work, and, because Bob cried whenever she went near him, it was Jeanne who had to look after him all the time.

Finally the Fisolles were the only visitors left in the house, which now looked as a house always does after a party, with dirty glasses and bottles all over the place and the rooms reeking of stale cigar smoke.

The train for Poitiers was at seven-forty. A little before seven, Jeanne, passing the drawing room, saw Roger Fisolle and his wife talking in an undertone, while Alice tried to divert the attention of her brother, who was sucking ice cream from a cone.

"Would you mind coming in a moment, Jeanne?" said Mme Fisolle, who had called her by her first name right from the start, though whether she regarded her as a relation or a servant it was impossible to tell. It looked more like the latter.

"Take your brother for a walk, Alice," she went on, "though mind you don't go far, since we shall have to be going soon."

And as they went out of the room she started to explain:

"Roger thought it might be better to wait till tomorrow, but there's still time to catch our train, and we haven't brought our things with us for the night."

As soon as the children were out of earshot she nodded

encouragingly to her husband, whose mustache smelled of wine and cigar smoke, and who, for a change, had now lit a pipe.

"But before you start, Roger, there's something I want to say to Jeanne. I want her to understand that, if we turn to her, it's because she's now the real mistress of the house. It wasn't necessary for Alice to tell us anything; we could see it at a glance. And between ourselves, it's a good thing, too. This morning I could have died of shame."

Jeanne stood there impassively. She was wearing her apron, for she had been helping Désirée on and off the whole day.

"Now, Roger—you go on."

Roger Fisolle puffed at his pipe, then cleared his throat.

"It's really quite simple," he began, "and I think it's only natural I should raise the question. I've had a few words with the chief clerk, who appears to be a most conscientious young man. But in his position, of course, he's not at liberty to say much. What I wanted to find out was when the family was going to be called to the notary's for the reading of the will. That is, if there is a will . . ."

Jeanne looked at him steadily, without showing the least surprise, but at the same time without giving him the least encouragement. Taking refuge in a businesslike tone, he went on:

"I don't know whether there was a marriage contract, but I have every reason to believe that the estate is a matter of joint ownership. However that may be, a portion of it is now due to come to the children. And in view of certain facts—of which the scene witnessed by my wife this morning was an example—in view of those facts I consider that the sooner the property gets into the hands of an executor the better it will be for everybody. Monsieur Sallenave was decidedly evasive, as indeed I expected, when I questioned him about the state of the business."

"Did you ask him if you could look at the books?"

He reddened, saying hastily:

71

"I didn't press him at all. Although I am myself more or less in the same line of business, I quite see that . . ."

"If I understand you rightly, what you want is for your daughter to receive her share of the estate at once. Is that it?"

It was the mother who answered. She spoke aggressively, barely able to control herself:

"Isn't it natural? You haven't been here long, but I take it you've seen quite enough to realize that this is a madhouse, to put it mildly. You may as well know, if you don't already, that we were dead against Alice's marrying Julien. We wanted her to get a degree, and when we sent her to the university, it wasn't with the idea of seeing her throw it up after her second year. . . .

"She was only a child, knowing nothing about life. He was four years older and ought to have known better. He none-theless took advantage of her ignorance at a moment of weakness. So that, if we agreed to the marriage in the end, it was because there was no other course.

"Now he's dead—God rest his soul!—and she has gone on living here because of the baby. But she has received neither the help nor the affection to which she was entitled. As for the example set her—you can judge that for yourself. No servant would stay in the house more than a few days. . . .

"Don't interrupt, Roger. I know what I'm saying. I'm well aware of the reproaches made against Alice. I'm not blind. I only had to keep my eyes open today to see the whole thing.

"What she's reproached with is not doing duty as a maid of all work. And I daresay she would have become one if I hadn't expressly told her not to. I didn't bring my daughter up to do the chores at home, and, if she hasn't done them for me, she's not going to do them for others.

"There are other things I might mention. If you know what I mean, so much the better. . . . In the meantime she'll go on staying here. After all, it's her home, isn't it?

"What I want you to realize is that she'll stand up for her rights. And now perhaps could we have an answer to the question my husband asked?"

"You want an immediate valuation for probate, I suppose?"

"Exactly. The important thing is to have everything valued and the business accounts audited by people who have no connection with the family here. Then there may be another question to go into, but we'll see about that later. And, having said that, I can only repeat that the sooner you take action the better. The future of a minor can't be left dependent on a woman who's not in full possession of her faculties, and who ought to be sent to some place where she'll be properly looked after."

"I see," said Jeanne simply. "I'll speak to Louise about it tomorrow, and the notary will keep you informed of developments."

Mme Fisolle opened the window to call Alice, who was standing on the sidewalk with the boy.

"Will you come to the station with us, Alice?"

And presently all four of them could be seen crossing the bridge and then hurrying as fast as they could along the main street, the boy dragging behind.

Like her mother, Madeleine had not reappeared during the day. Jeanne hadn't been surprised. As for Henri, he had, so to speak, undergone his baptism of fire. Now that he was the head of the house, everybody had made a point of treating him with a touch of deference, and at one moment Jeanne had caught sight of him smoking a cigar in the middle of a group of men. He had ceremoniously seen each of his guests off the premises, though toward the end his gait had been just a little unsteady.

"Désirée! Do you know where Henri's got to?"

"Suppose you stop bothering about the others for a moment! Since first thing this morning I haven't seen you sit down once, except to give the baby his bottle."

"And what about you?"

"Oh! I'm used to it."

As she spoke an idea crossed her mind. It wasn't lost on Jeanne, and she noticed that from that moment her former schoolfellow looked at her with something like a tinge of suspicion in her eyes. But she went on:

"You'd better go and lie down for a while, and tomorrow morning . . ."

"First, I want to know what Henri's doing."

She went upstairs, noticing that Madeleine had resumed possession of her room. The door was locked. Henri wasn't anywhere. Then, going down again, she saw that a light was on in the office.

She crossed the yard and opened the glass-paneled door. There was the boy, sitting at the office desk, his head in his arms, crying his eyes out. He too smelled of drink. When she touched his shoulder, he raised his head, but didn't shrug her off.

"Have they gone?" he asked in a melodramatic voice, struggling against his tears.

"Yes. They've all gone now."

"What a ghastly business," he sneered. "They came to bury my father, who was their relation or their friend, and no sooner have they got through the business than they settle down to eat and drink, smoking his cigars and stuffing some away in their pockets. And they finish up by telling dirty stories. Poor Father! Meanwhile, Mother . . ."

"Leave her alone, Henri."

"As a matter of fact, I haven't the right to throw stones. Where was I when my father died? What was I doing? And here I am sitting at the desk where my grandfather worked and feeling that I'm utterly worthless. Today they've all been slapping me on the back saying:

" 'You're a man now, Henri, and we expect great things of you.' "

Because of all the wine he'd drunk, the world must have appeared to him as though under a magnifying glass. Everything was exaggerated, and his own feelings, his voice, his gestures were exaggerated in the same proportion.

"You're strong, you are, Aunt Jeanne. That's why everyone hates you. Even me. At least I try to. You see, you haven't the

74

same little meannesses we have, and it makes us feel cheap."

"Do you really believe that?" she asked, almost laughing.

"As for me, I'm rotten to the core. I suppose I take after Mother. Mad despises her, but I daresay it's not her fault. Is it her fault, Aunt Jeanne, that she's like that?"

"No, Henri."

"And is it my fault that I'm made like this? Do you think I'll ever be capable of growing up into a man like my father? Perhaps you think it was out of cowardice that he killed himself. There were some of them today who hinted it was because he was in a jam over money."

"No one knows the reason."

"Not even you?"

"Not even me."

"Were you fond of him?"

"Yes."

"Perhaps I'll get fond of you too."

Suddenly ashamed of his demonstrativeness, he tried to pass it off with a sneer.

"You see. I'm beginning to talk like Mother. I'd do better to keep my mouth shut."

"Come."

"All right."

The fresh air outside must have upset him, for, in a voice that had become childish again, he said:

"I think I'll take a breath of air. You go in."

It wasn't quite dark, but when Jeanne looked back out of the kitchen window he was no more than a shadowy figure, and she couldn't be quite sure he was being sick at the foot of the lime tree.

"Won't you really rest for a bit?"

"Not until the house looks something like its normal self again."

And she set to work, not unaware of Désirée's puzzled glances behind her back. The truth was that if she once stopped, she'd never have the strength to start again. It had

75

been like that for the last three days, and she sometimes wondered how it was she had felt so tired on her arrival. And to think that on the platform at Poitiers she had actually held her hands to her chest thinking she was going to die! It seemed to her now quite incredible.

Since then she hadn't had a moment's respite. If she did sit down for a few minutes' rest, someone was sure to bob up wanting this or that, the baby would start crying, the telephone would ring, or the milk would boil over on the stove. Or, to tell the truth, it might be something within herself, an imperious urge to forge blindly ahead, keeping the spring at full tension.

"Has Bob kept quiet?"

"Yes."

"Hasn't his mother come in yet?"

Alice didn't get back till nine. She offered no explanation. Probably she had run into a boy on the way home, for her face was flushed and her lipstick slightly smudged.

"I'm not hungry," she announced. "We've had too much to eat today. I'm going up to bed."

"Good night, Alice."

She couldn't have helped noticing that the two women were up to their eyes in work, but she pretended not to.

"What about you, Henri? Isn't it about time you went up too?"

He had been wandering about gloomily from room to room, feeling a bit queasy in the stomach. From time to time he stood watching Jeanne and Désirée. Several times, as though absent-mindedly, he had carried something to the kitchen, a glass or an ashtray that had been overlooked.

"I'll go to bed soon."

"Come up with me," said Alice. "There's something I want to tell you."

He was rather embarrassed by her mysterious and inviting manner, and it was obvious to everybody she wanted to talk of some amorous adventure. He went just the same, not knowing quite how to refuse. When he said good night to

Jeanne, it was in an offhand tone, as he was shy of betraying any feeling. On account of Bob, he took Alice into his room and shut the door.

"Well, maybe we'll get a little peace now," sighed Désirée. It was curious. Though educated at the same convent school as Jeanne, she seemed to have slipped quite easily into the attitude and even into the mentality of a servant. Even toward her old friend, her manner had changed perceptibly in the course of these three days. She had dropped some of her familiarity, and even more lost some of her frankness. Admittedly she still called Jeanne by her first name and would now and again make a grimace behind Louise's back expressing either sarcasm or irritation. But, obliged to work for others, she had ended by growing into the part. It was otherwise with Jeanne. It was all very well for her to go about all day in an apron and put her hand to everything, even the dirtiest jobs; she was nonetheless the virtual mistress of the house. Désirée couldn't make her out. In her eyes, Jeanne was neither one thing nor the other.

Her question about Bob just now had set Désirée thinking. She was puzzled. They were both at the sink, up to their elbows in soapy water, washing piles of plates worthy of a restaurant. It was quite obvious Désirée had something on her mind but didn't know quite how to broach the subject. Finally she came out with:

"Do you like children?"

"Very much. Particularly the little ones."

"It's funny. You've never had any, yet you go about the job as if you'd been doing it for years. You've got a way with you that many a mother of a family might envy. Have you had much practice?"

"Yes."

"Ah! I daresay your husband had brothers and sisters married. Though I thought you'd spent your life in hot countries."

"I have, more or less. But they have children in hot countries, just the same as we do. As a matter of fact, I was

77

looking after children for three years. I worked as a nurse in a family with five children. The eldest was ten when I left."

"I didn't know. I always thought Lauer was rich, and imagined he'd left you plenty of money."

"No."

"Was that in South America?"

"In Egypt. Not far from Cairo. I was in a Belgian family. The husband was an engineer in a sugar refinery."

"Did they treat you well?"

Jeanne didn't answer. The plates followed each other in quick succession, making a familiar clatter. From time to time she lifted an arm to wipe her eyes, for the steam condensed on her eyelashes.

"Why did you leave?"

"It was they who left."

"They went back to Belgium? Why didn't they take you with them?"

"It would have been too expensive for them, paying my fare. It was at the beginning of the war."

"What did you do after that? Excuse me. I oughtn't to ask such questions. For my part, I'm not in the least ashamed. Everyone knows all about it. My husband was shot for trafficking with the Germans and all his property was confiscated. For a long time nobody wanted to give me a job of any sort. With you it's different."

"Yes, it's different. It was my own wish."

"What was? I don't understand."

"I left because I'd decided to."

"Left home? That's what you're talking about, is it? You mean when you were a girl?"

"When I was twenty-one. Exactly twenty-one. The very day I came of age."

"I didn't know. I heard you left because your father wouldn't let you marry Lauer."

"That's true. More or less."

"Did you ever make it up with him?"

"I never saw him again."

"Didn't you mind being so far away, cut off from your family?"

"For a while I corresponded with Robert, who kept me informed."

"Do you think he was unhappy with his wife?"

"I don't know."

"I must say, I was sorry for her this morning. Of course she oughtn't to have got into that state, but it didn't give her daughter the right to treat her that way. Particularly in public, and on a day like this. By the way, I've found out where she keeps the stuff. Do you know where your sister-in-law was when you were looking for her? In the bathroom halfway up the stairs, the one nobody uses. Behind the door, there's a door in the wall, low down. I don't really know what it's for. A sort of cupboard."

Jeanne remembered it well, but neither did she know what purpose it had ever served. She had hidden things in it herself as a child, when she played with her brothers.

"I guess she's been using it for a long time. The empty bottle was outside, near the sink, but inside there were three full bottles as well as two empties. It's not wine she drinks, but spirits. Cognac and armagnac. My mother-in-law had hiding places too, but in her case it was money that she hid away from her husband and her children."

Another hour's work—two at the most—and the house would once again be clean and tidy.

"You're not thinking of washing the floor at this time of night?"

"Yes."

"What for?"

"So that, when they come down in the morning, they'll find everything just as usual. Perhaps I'm fussy, but I can't help feeling it matters. I suppose I'm like the English. They say they dress for dinner even in the desert."

"Have you seen them?"

"Not in the desert. In Egypt, yes. And the Argentine."

She spoke halfheartedly, her real thoughts elsewhere, and

Désirée could never have guessed what images were being conjured up in her mind.

They heard a faint sound on the landing upstairs, and both of them had the same reflex: to look up at the ceiling, as though they could see through it. Then they turned toward the door, to find Henri standing there. He was in pajamas and robe, his hair rumpled, as though he'd been to bed, but he was wide awake and agitated.

"Aunt Jeanne, Mad's packing."

"How do you know?"

"After leaving Alice, I went to say good night to her. I could see a light under the door, but she wouldn't open it. Not thinking anything of it, I went to bed. Through the wall, I heard her moving about, and that kept me from going to sleep. She was opening and shutting drawers one after the other, and then she dragged something heavy along the floor and I realized it was a trunk. She must have brought it down from the top floor this afternoon when nobody was upstairs. I went back and told her to open the door or I'd come and tell you. Finally she let me in.

"She's almost ready. Her traveling coat's on the bed. I asked her where she was thinking of going and she told me that was no business of mine."

"Did you try to stop her?"

"I told her she was crazy, that she had no right to do a thing like that, that she had nowhere to go and no money."

"What did she say to that?"

"The same thing. That it had nothing to do with me."

"Did she give any explanation?"

He reddened, and she realized she mustn't ask him to betray his sister.

"She mustn't go, Aunt Jeanne. There are things you don't know. If she went, it would be terrible—and it would be my fault."

"You're great friends?"

"We were. For a while."

"You used to go out together?"

He looked away, as though guessing what was in her mind. "Yes."

"How long ago was that?"

"Two years. Nearly two years."

"Come with me."

She led him into the little living room they called the *petit salon*, which opened onto the hall. It was furnished in Louis XVI style, lit by wall fittings in the form of candles. He had followed her reluctantly, and he was crimson now, as though he was facing an ordeal that he had long dreaded. Standing with his hands in the pockets of his robe, he stared at the floor.

"There are one or two questions I want to ask you, strictly between ourselves, because if we're going to keep Mad from going, there are some things I must know. Or perhaps it would be better for me to lead off by telling you what I think. You can stop me if I'm wrong."

"But she'll be coming down in a minute."

"She can't leave the house without passing that door. We're bound to see her. When Madeleine started going out with you two years ago, you were seventeen. So she was fifteen. I imagine that at that time you weren't taking your father's car."

"No."

"Where did you go?"

"To the movies, or for a ride in a friend's car."

"Your friends were older than you then?"

"Yes."

"The other day you were two boys with two girls. I suppose it was much the same two years ago. And I daresay your sister wanted to behave with other boys the way the girls you took out behaved with you."

"I didn't want her to."

"I can well believe it. And it was because you showed your disapproval that she started going off on her own."

"That was about a year ago."

"Do you know her friends?"

"Not all."

"I wouldn't mind betting they're not boys of your age."

"No. They're not."

His ears were burning. He must have been going through the worst experience in all his life, one that had often haunted him in nightmares.

"They're older men, aren't they? Married men, most likely. And somewhere in Mad's room there are things hidden away, presents they've given her, and which she didn't want her parents to see."

"How did you know?"

"That's all, Henri. You can go back to bed now. Or, if you're afraid Mad will reproach you for coming to tell me, you can stay down here. Only, when she comes down, you must leave us alone together."

"I'm wondering now whether I did right in telling you."

"You did quite right."

"Of course, you're bound to say so, but . . ."

She was crossing the hall to go back to help Désirée when he overtook her and plucked her by the sleeve. This time he was thoroughly worried. Since they were within earshot of the kitchen, he begged her in a shaky voice:

"Come back a moment, will you?"

She followed him back into the room they had left, and he led her over to the farthest corner, where he stood for a while in silence, not daring to look her in the face. He was trying to pluck up his courage to tell her something. But it was hard, very hard, and she didn't know how to help him. Finally, wringing his hands, he stammered in an almost inaudible voice:

"It didn't happen quite as I told you just now."

"You didn't tell me anything. It's I who did the talking."

He pricked up his ears, terrified at the thought of Mad coming down and having a talk with his aunt before he'd had time to speak.

"At that time—two years ago—I used to make fun of her."

"Why?"

82

"Because she always stayed at home all by herself, or, if she did go out with friends, they were frightful bores. When I came home, I made a point of telling her what a good time I'd had, even when it wasn't true."

"Did you tell her everything?"

"Not everything."

"I understand."

"At least, not at first. But I told her she was a silly little prig and would end up an old maid."

"She was fifteen."

"I know. I was a fool. I didn't realize then what I was doing."

"You may as well admit that it's only today that you've realized what a girl is."

"Perhaps you're right. . . . Then she started asking me why I didn't take her with me."

"What did you answer?"

"That that sort of thing wasn't for her, wasn't for sisters."

"Did she understand?"

"No. But I told her she had never let a boy kiss her, and that we all did in our crowd. I don't know why I said that. I seemed to have an itch to talk to her about that sort of thing. I mentioned one or two of my girlfriends who were only too ready to go the whole way. She was indignant, refused to believe it, and said I was lying. Then I gave her details."

"All the details?"

"Pretty well. All except the smuttiest. After that, it was she who got in the habit of questioning me. When I came back late, I'd find her in my room, sitting in the dark, waiting for me. One day she said:

" 'I want you to take me with you next Sunday.'

"I was surprised. I tried to talk her out of it.

" 'You know what they'll expect of you, don't you?'

" 'But you say all my friends do it.'

" 'Not all.'

" 'Most of them, then. It comes to the same thing.'

"No one has ever known anything about that, Aunt

Jeanne, and I tell you it's often kept me awake at night. I felt sure it would end badly. Every time I think of it I get shivers down my back.

"I can't think how I could have done it. Of course I was only a kid. . . ."

She didn't smile.

"In the end I agreed. I took her along. But I give you my word, I didn't really believe she would do like the others did. One always has the feeling a sister's different."

"But it wasn't different," said Jeanne quietly.

"No. And it's I who was ashamed. There were some of my friends I stopped going with because of that. She too was ashamed, I think, but only on my account, and she decided to go off on her own in the future. During this last year I've known practically nothing about her movements. When she comes in, she looks at me sarcastically. Sometimes, particularly in the morning, I feel she hates me. That's why she mustn't go. It's all my fault. If she goes, I think I'll end by doing like Father."

"Tell me, Henri, did your father know?"

"About Mad?"

He hesitated once again. Then:

"One Sunday morning, when I hadn't gone to mass and Mad was out, I saw the door of her room open as I was going down to get some breakfast. My father was there. As soon as he saw me, he quickly shut a drawer and pretended to be busy with something else. He muttered something awkwardly—I don't remember what. I had noticed which drawer it was, and a little later I went to explore. Underneath some underwear was one of those things women use."

He didn't know which way to look.

"Did your father speak to her about it?"

"I don't know. I doubt it. Anyhow she went on just as before."

"He didn't speak to you either?"

"About Mad?"

"About yourself."

"He did try once, early on."

"And then?"

"Perhaps he realized it was no use. Perhaps . . ."

"Perhaps what?"

Tears filled his eyes and ran down his cheeks. He didn't bother to wipe them away, and they no doubt soothed him a bit.

"I don't know. I've been thinking about it all the time these last few days. I often wondered why he wasn't stricter. To my friends I always boasted of having a marvelous father. Perhaps he was afraid we might run away, Mad and I. Or . . . or that we might stop being fond of him . . ."

For the first time, through his warm tears, he looked her straight in the face, and one might have thought he was on the point of throwing himself on her bosom. And what was that glint in his eye? A tiny spark of joy?

For fear of softening too much, he went on in a slightly derisive tone:

"And now it's my turn to be afraid of Mad running away! So scared that I've come running to you to blurt out all our filthy secrets. For that's what they are, aren't they? If you only knew how I loathed myself! Do you still think you'll be able to stop her?"

"Hush!"

A door opened upstairs. There was no attempt to do it quietly; in fact, the precaution would have been useless in view of the noise that followed, for a trunk was dragged across the landing and down the stairs, bumping on each step in turn.

Jeanne left Henri and closed the door behind her. Then she took a position at the bottom of the stairs and stood watching Madeleine. The latter, in a checked traveling coat, held onto the banister rail with one hand while with the other she held a handle of the trunk to prevent it from sliding down the stairs. She came down step by step with a little pause on each.

Mad betrayed neither surprise nor annoyance at finding

her aunt there. She came on, and at each step the trunk gave a jolt to her arm.

She took her time, absorbed in what she was doing, the tip of her tongue between her lips. The moment was approaching when they would come face to face and one of them would have to give way. Jeanne shut the kitchen door, making it quite clear that there were just the two of them to measure their strength against each other.

Eight steps more, then seven . . . Three, two, and finally the trunk bumped onto the mat at the bottom. With a final effort she managed to pull it up onto its end, without Jeanne making a movement to help her.

Mad's lips quivered slightly, but her eyes were steady, as she at last faced Jeanne, who, in the most natural way in the world, asked:

"Have you called for a taxi?"

"There's no point. I'll find one outside the hotel."

"It's true. There should be one there."

She let her pass and, throwing off her apron, followed. Mad heard her footsteps behind her, but it was only at the entrance that she turned around.

"Where are you going?"

And, as though it was the most natural thing in the world, Jeanne answered:

"I'm coming with you. To find a taxi."

6

She had a dream that she had already had before, at the age of eleven or twelve, when she was laid up with mumps. With the rest of the family she was staying in a boardinghouse at the seaside, during the summer vacation. She had the feeling she had suddenly become monstrously fat, fat enough to fill up a whole room. What was so horrible was that her flesh was soft and spongy like that of some fungus, and so light that she could have floated in the air.

It wasn't entirely a dream, for she was conscious of being in her own room and her own bed. It had been just the same the first time. Then, it had been the boardinghouse bedroom; this time, it was her room at home, the same she had had as a girl, though the blue-and-pink-flowered wallpaper was gone, replaced by a modern one of neutral tint and no pattern at all. Gone too was the big mahogany bed whose smooth surface she had loved to stroke. In its place was a low couch with practically no woodwork showing at all. In fact, the only piece of furniture left from the old days was a humble little chest of drawers with a broken leg that had been stuck on again. By some miracle it had been spared, and still stood between the windows.

No doubt all the old furniture—and heaven knows there was a mass of it—had been sold at auction. Somebody must have bought the little table she had transformed into a dressing table. She had always longed for a real dressing table, and at fifteen, since they still refused to buy her one, she had improvised one herself out of a plain pine table, around which she had fixed cretonne flounces hanging right down to the floor. On it she had stood a triple mirror, whose frame she had painted gray. Her brothers had laughed at it, calling it her crinoline.

She couldn't very well have mumps this time, since she'd had them already. It would certainly have been ridiculous if she had. At her age! Like old Mme Dubois of the umbrella shop, who had had whooping cough at sixty-eight, and died of it.

People used to ask her husband, on purpose:

"What did she die of?"

"Of whooping cough."

It sounded so funny that it was all one could do not to burst out laughing.

Jeanne had set the alarm for six o'clock. She could remember that in her sleep. She could hear it ticking. It was important that it should go off at the right time, because she knew the day was to be of crucial importance. That's why it mattered so much, her being all swollen up.

She couldn't remember why the day was to be so important. But she soon would when she got up in the morning. So long as she hadn't fallen ill! *Mon Dieu!* That was an awful thought!

She sank back for a while into a heavy, turbid sleep, then floated up to the surface again, recovering consciousness of the passing hours, of the never-ending night, and of the remorseless ticking of the clock. When at last the alarm sounded, bringing deliverance, she had known for some time that it was daylight. In fact, she had known almost to a second when the bell would start ringing.

She was in her bed all right, and it was indeed her own room up on the third floor. The sun was up, shining through the yellow blind. A locomotive whistled at the station. But all at once the feeling of deliverance vanished, and she threw back the covers to look at her legs, which lay painfully heavy on the mattress.

She might have known this would happen. The doctors had warned her about it. In fact, she'd had it before, though, except for the first time, the attacks had been much milder and had come on gradually.

During the night her legs had swollen to such an extent that all trace of the knees had been obliterated. The flesh was smooth, the color of candles, and it was difficult to recognize it as her own. If she pressed on it with a finger, it made a hollow and a still whiter patch, which only slowly disappeared.

The trouble was she knew now why the day was of such importance, and why, the evening before, in spite of Désirée's ill-concealed annoyance, she had insisted on having everything spick-and-span before coming up to bed.

The first thing was to find out whether she could get on her feet, which were as swollen as her legs. If she could, she might at least go downstairs, if only to sit in a chair all day. But there was no question of putting on slippers, let alone shoes.

Cautiously, imploring the fates, she put one foot, then the other, down onto the mat beside her bed, and helping herself with her hands, just managed to stand up, painful though it was. But she knew at once that she couldn't take a single step without falling down. She dared not even try, because she could picture herself lying helpless on the floor in her nightgown, with her hair down her back, raising all the household with her cries for help.

Once again sitting on the edge of the bed, she almost wept. On the floor below everyone was certain to be still asleep.

Désirée was more doubtful. She was of farming stock, used to early rising, and she spent precious little time dressing, in a hurry as she always was for her first cup of coffee.

Supposing Désirée was down already? What would Jeanne do then? The rooms at the top of the house weren't provided with bells. Knowing her to have gone to bed late and very tired, they might leave her alone for hours before coming up. She listened intently for any sound. Désirée's room was on the other side of the passage; she had herself chosen one of the servants' rooms which looked out onto the yard.

For a good ten minutes she heard nothing. She wondered whether she oughtn't to drag herself to the door, on all fours if necessary, to be sure of catching the maid as she passed. But she hardly dared move, fearing to make a noise herself that might prevent her hearing other sounds.

Fortunately, Désirée had gone to bed just as late as she had, well after midnight. At last she heard a faucet running and soft steps, and she knew she hadn't much longer to wait.

"Désirée!" she called in a muffled voice, as soon as she heard a door open.

She held one of her slippers in her hand, ready to fling it against the door as a signal if her voice didn't carry.

"Désirée!"

The steps stopped, then started again.

"Désirée!"

The latter at last turned around and came back, stopping outside the door to listen, in case she'd been mistaken.

"Come in. The door's not locked."

Her friend looked at her questioningly, with a slightly bewildered expression on her face, as though this was the last thing in the world she had expected.

"What's the matter? Aren't you feeling well?"

She hadn't noticed the swollen feet, and Jeanne, who was still sitting on the edge of the bed, quickly tucked them away under the covers.

"Come in and shut the door. And don't talk too loud. Now listen to me. As far as I'm concerned, there's nothing to worry about. I've had this trouble three or four times in the last few years and it always passes in a few days. Only, you must call Dr. Bernard, sometime about eight o'clock, I should think, before he starts out on his rounds, and ask him to come and see me. Send him right up, and if you can smuggle him up without anybody seeing, so much the better."

"I told you you were overdoing it."

"I know. But it was necessary and I'm glad to know it's done. Still, we won't go into that now. The only thing that worries me is that I'm going to be terribly dependent on you for the next few days, and I don't know how your legs are going to stand it—what with all these stairs."

"Don't worry. I'll nurse you. I'm used to it. With my husband . . ."

"There won't be any nursing to do. The doctor will give me some medicine, and we'll just have to wait for it to act. It's not even painful. The important thing today is for me to be kept informed of all that goes on downstairs. This is, so to speak, their first day. Do you understand? And the future depends on it."

"Yes, I think I understand. Only, I think you take a lot too much trouble over people who . . ."

"I want you to do exactly what I tell you, and I'm asking it as a personal favor."

"For you, of course, I'd do anything."

"Well, first of all, you've got to be in a good humor. I don't mean that you've got to be laughing and singing all day long. But I want them, as soon as they come down, to feel that the tension has ceased. Take extra trouble over the breakfast. Lay the table nicely. Try to get some croissants and serve them hot. You've time to slip around to the baker's."

"Do you really think they're going to sit down all together to a family breakfast?"

"It doesn't matter whether they do or not. The thing is to lay the table as though it was a matter of course. Put each person's napkin in its place. And perhaps you'd better lay a place for me too."

"If that's what you want . . ."

Evidently it was too complicated for her.

"Bob's bound to cry, and no matter what you think of his mother, do your best to soothe him, because when he yells he gets everybody's nerves on edge. For that matter, you could bring him up to me, if you don't know what else to do with him. I can't get up, but I could feed him here on my bed and keep him amused."

"Is that all?"

"Not quite. When Monsieur Sallenave arrives—it's generally about half past eight—I want you to give him a message from me. And make sure no one else is around."

"You want him to come up and see you?"

"By no means. Not unless it's absolutely necessary. On the contrary, I want him to wait till Henri's had his breakfast and then seek him out, telling him, as if it was quite natural, that he needs his help. He can trump up something for him to do; it doesn't matter what. And he can discuss the business with him and ask his advice on one or two little matters. The important thing is to make him sit down in his father's chair."

"All right. Though I doubt very much whether it'll work, and once again I tell you you're taking a lot of pains for . . ."

"One thing more. There'll be a telephone call to put through after my sister-in-law has been up to see me."

"Do you think she'll come?"

"Perhaps. And then you'll call up Monsieur Bigeois, the notary, and tell him Robert Martineau's sister would like to see him, but that unfortunately she's confined to her bed."

"Is that all?"

"Yes."

"What'll you have to eat?"

"It doesn't matter. Perhaps I'd better have nothing, since I won't be allowed anything with salt in it."

"I can make you something specially."

"Nonsense. You've enough to do without that. Now run along, my poor Désirée. I hope it won't be for long. It's only today that I want you to come up as often as you can. By tomorrow things will have got into a new groove. It's the thought of *your* legs that worries me. Now, if you'll just pass me that comb, a wet washcloth, and the eau de Cologne that's on the chest of drawers. The room already smells of illness. When I'm like this I can't bear my own smell, so I can guess what it's like for others!"

It was a very strange day indeed. She had thought a lot about it before going to sleep the previous night, trying to foresee all the possibilities, so that she might be ready to meet whatever came. She knew they would wake up feeling awkward and ashamed, even angry with themselves, as after a sordid binge, and in such a mood everything was tricky, each word, each gesture a possible pitfall, the mere fact of sitting down to a meal or looking in this direction rather than that.

That's why she had wanted to put everything straight the night before, so that the house itself would be inviting, and she had counted on being there to ensure—unobtrusively of course—that every cause of friction was avoided.

Instead of that, here she was, chained to her bed right up at the top of the house, with no contact with the rest of the world but through the good offices of Désirée—and Désirée, whatever she might promise, would be only too ready to put on a sour face in revenge for all the extra work she had had to do the day before.

The first signs of life came from the town, in the distance, over by the station. At eight came a loud noise from behind the house when the foreman opened the big doors of the warehouse, then the rumble of empty barrels being rolled across the courtyard.

It was then that Désirée came up for the first time, bringing *café au lait* and some bread and butter that Jeanne didn't touch.

"What shall I tell them when they ask me what's the matter with you?"

"That I'm a bit overtired, but will be coming down later."

"But that's not true."

"Never mind. Say it just the same. How is it I haven't heard a sound from Bob this morning?"

"When his mother came down to warm up the milk for his bottle, she had him in her arms. I offered to look after him, but she said she'd see to him herself. As I came up, she was humming a tune to him."

She had no doubt been warned by her parents to be on her best behavior, so as not to provide material for a counter-attack.

"You'd better get his playpen set up. But put it in the dining room, where he can see people occasionally. In the little room next door, he looks as if he's been put out of the way."

"It'll take up a lot of room."

"Just so. Make it as obvious as possible."

"If that's what you want."

Surprisingly, Louise was the first down. Jeanne had told Désirée to leave her door open, and she could hear her sister-in-law stop and listen at the top of the stairs before taking the plunge.

Next, she heard Henri going into the dining room, and a moment later the doctor knocking on the front door. There was no question now of his coming up unobserved. For a minute or two he spoke to someone, she couldn't tell whom, then she heard his firm step on the stairs. As he approached, he paused for a moment discreetly, before appearing in the doorway.

"Can I come in?"

"Please do."

He was as calm and cool as ever. Since six o'clock, Jeanne's left eyelid had had time to swell up. It looked like a bee sting, but he wasn't taken in for a moment, and, bringing up a chair, he promptly set about taking her blood pressure.

"It's not the first time?"

"No. It happened to me in Egypt ten years ago. Then three or four times in Istanbul."

"Let's see your legs."

He felt them, made her move her toes, then pulled the covers up again.

"Have you had your heart examined recently?"

"Two months ago. Just before leaving. I was told it wasn't in too bad shape and that I had nothing to worry about from that quarter. Did my sister-in-law speak to you?"

"I didn't see her. Only her son."

"Did he know you were here on my account?"

"It would have been difficult to hide it."

"What's he like this morning?"

"Calm. A bit haggard."

"Did he say anything to you?"

"He asked me not to leave without seeing him again."

He sighed as he put back his stethoscope.

"You know the diet?"

"No salt. Very little meat. No spices. No tea or coffee. And every two hours take one of the pills you're going to give me, with a large glass of water."

She smiled at him.

"There's one other thing—the most important."

"I know. Not to put my feet on the ground."

"Will it be all right if I give the prescription to your maid? Or would you rather I had the stuff sent right from a druggist's?"

"That would be better, if you don't mind. She's got a lot on her hands as it is, and with me in the bargain . . . Tell me, Doctor, how long do you think it will be?"

"How long were you laid up last time?"

"A week, but . . ."

"Then you'd better allow two. Perhaps a little less."

He hadn't stopped studying her since he came in, with the same keen scrutiny as on Sunday, but this time she had the feeling he was on the brink of thawing. Indeed, as he made for the door, he almost turned around, but in the end merely announced:

"I'll be calling in again tomorrow."

While he was there, it was impossible for Jeanne to follow

the sounds below as closely as she would have wished—
enough, however, for the doctor to notice it. She was quite
sure of that. And it was then that he was most tempted to
speak to her.

He didn't stay long downstairs. Almost immediately, she
heard the front door. From Désirée's steps as she came and
went and from the clatter of dishes, she gathered that most of
the family were now at breakfast together.

Another half hour went by before anyone came up. Again
it was Désirée, who made an obvious effort not to appear out
of breath.

"What did he say?" she asked, sitting down on the edge of
a chair.

"What I knew he would—that it is nothing to worry
about."

"No salt."

"Neither salt nor pepper. That is, if you can find the time.
What are they doing downstairs?"

"First of all, I saw Monsieur Sallenave, as you said, and he
seemed to understand at once. He came and got Henri a few
minutes ago."

"Who's in the dining room? I heard my sister-in-law go
down. Did she talk to you?"

"When she came down, she looked more like a ghost than
a living person, and she crept about so quietly that I didn't
notice her right away. She looked as if she was afraid of
someone, and all ready to bolt back into her room if anyone
said a cross word to her. She looked into the kitchen on her
way to the dining room and seemed surprised not to see you
there. I immediately brought her some nice hot coffee, so she
had nothing to do but sit down and drink it.

" 'Isn't my sister-in-law down?' she asked.

"I told her just what you said, and at that moment Henri
appeared. I gave him his coffee too. He didn't look at his
mother but mumbled a vague good morning. Then I went
back with the croissants, which I'd warmed up, as you
wanted me to. And then . . . wait a minute. With all these

96

comings and goings, it's difficult to get things sorted out. And as soon as I try to remember I get all muddled up. . . .

"Oh, yes. The doctor. He came then. I dashed to the front door, and might have got him past without anyone knowing if Henri hadn't come into the hall to see who it was. They talked for a while together. Then, while the doctor was up here with you, Alice came down, all washed and dressed and with her hair fixed. She was carrying Bob, and as soon as she saw the playpen she tried putting him in it. He began by crying, but I went and played with him for a bit so that Alice could have her breakfast, and he soon got used to it and let me go back to my work."

"Did they talk to each other?"

"Not much. I think Henri said something about you and the doctor. Then the doctor came down again, cold as an iceberg, as always, and Henri jumped up and saw him out, following him onto the sidewalk."

"That's why I didn't hear them."

"Henri came in through the back door, and told me to bring you your medicine the moment it came. Also to make you some special food without salt or pepper. He was most concerned about it. He went back into the dining room, and through the open door I could see him giving the news to the others with an air of self-importance.

"And a few minutes ago, as I said, Monsieur Sallenave came in through the kitchen looking serious, and said out loud:

" 'Is Monsieur Henri here?'

" 'He's in the dining room.'

" 'Do you think I might bother him?'

" 'Of course.'

"I didn't follow him, since I wasn't sure I could keep a straight face. They came out through the kitchen together and, as he passed me, the boy said:

" 'Will you tell my aunt I meant to come up at once to see how she was, but Monsieur Sallenave wants to see me about something important. As soon as I get a chance I'll go up to

97

her. See that she looks after herself. On no account must she get up.' "

"Is that all?" asked Jeanne, who was only half reassured, but who couldn't help laughing all the same. "What's my sister-in-law doing with herself?"

"She goes hither and thither like an insect that doesn't quite know where it wants to be. Once or twice she's stopped in front of Bob in his playpen, which she can't miss, since it's right in everyone's way. But she hasn't yet made up her mind to play with him."

"Alice?"

"Still eating. Reading the paper."

"And Madeleine?"

"She hasn't shown up yet. But I heard sounds as I passed her room just now. Shall I telephone Monsieur Bigeois?"

"Not just yet. Wait till I tell you."

"Won't you eat anything?"

"For lunch, if you have time, you can cook me some vegetables. Some French beans would do, if you've got any in the house. . . . Has anyone called?"

"No."

"Well, thank you, Désirée."

"It's nothing. You'd better try to sleep. I'll shut the door."

"Don't do that. Not on any account!"

And as soon as the other had gone she pricked up her ears once again, leaning across the bed so that she could hear better. She realized that for Mad it was harder than for the others, and that she was putting off the moment when she had to go down. It was Mad she was worried about.

Fortunately, not only was her trunk unpacked, but Jeanne and Désirée had lugged it up to the top floor. It was now safely stowed away in a neighboring room, used for trunks and lumber of all sorts.

For Désirée that business of the trunk had been just about the last straw. It was after midnight, and Jeanne was almost afraid she'd refuse to help with it.

"Do you think it makes sense, dragging the thing up to the

98

top of the house in the middle of the night when there's plenty of room for it everywhere?"

Oh, yes! It made sense, all right, and was in fact of the utmost importance. Mad had understood that.

Jeanne and her niece had hardly exchanged a word, and it was a silent walk that they had taken through the dark streets of the town.

It was a far more ticklish moment than this morning, and a single misplaced word might have ruined everything. In all her life, Jeanne had never looked so serene or been so tense inside as when she crossed the bridge beside the girl on whom she was inflicting her company.

Mad walked with long, firm strides, looking straight in front of her, determined to ignore the fact that she was not alone. She seemed to be saying:

"Come with me if you like. I can't stop you, since the sidewalk belongs to all, but you're merely wasting your time."

She was still in the first flush of revolt, and full of self-confidence. The first rebuff came when, contrary to her expectations, by some miraculous chance, there was no taxi outside the Anneau d'Or.

She stopped dead a few yards from the terrace, taking care to keep in the shadow, perhaps because she was shy of being seen in a gay checked coat on the night of her father's funeral.

A few people were still sitting there over their drinks, enjoying the evening coolness. A young woman in shorts, smoking a cigarette, was leaning back in her wicker armchair with one leg crossed over the other in such a way that there wasn't much you couldn't see. She laughed incessantly, exasperatingly, as she blew clouds of smoke at the two men sitting in front of her. Through the wide-open windows, in a haze of smoke, the regular customers could be seen playing cards, some of them, no doubt, men whom Jeanne had known as boys.

"There doesn't seem anything else to do but go and

try to find one at the station," suggested Jeanne blandly.

Blandly, yes. But she took the utmost care not to let the least hint of sarcasm creep into her voice. The thing was to get Mad going on again. The one thing she didn't want her to do was to turn back to the house and order a taxi by telephone.

The woman on the terrace had something so aggressive about her, something so revolting in her pose and in her laugh, that it was perhaps in a spirit of unconscious defiance that Mad decided to move on.

They walked on through alternating light and dark patches as they approached or receded from a streetlight. A man, a workman probably, off to some night job, kept abreast of them on the opposite sidewalk, and the ring of his heels on the flagstones accompanied them all the way.

Jeanne said nothing. Neither did Mad, who walked on, looking neither right nor left, her hands thrust deep into her pockets.

Her aunt, on the contrary, was interested in her surroundings. She looked at the houses, and the shops, most of which were shuttered, but whose names she could read. A bank with a façade of white concrete stood in the place of two shops she had known, the hat shop of the Cairel sisters and the umbrella shop of that old Mme Dubois who had died of whooping cough. So many she had known were dead now. There must be a whole quarter of the cemetery occupied by them. And most of the shopkeepers of today would be there too by the time Madeleine reached her age.

Then there would no doubt be some other Désirée to say to her in a voice as monotonous as a dripping faucet:

"Do you remember Germaine Doncoeur? The girl who was so freckled that she looked like a loaf of bread? She's married now, with seven children, but still carries on with her parents' shop. Her eldest daughter married our deputy and one of her sons is a colonial governor."

The street was long, rising gently. They passed a hotel which Jeanne had known as a scrubby little place with an evil reputation, but which had now been renamed and freshly painted.

It was her silence, she knew very well, that disconcerted her niece and made her step less assured. But the battle was not yet over, and she held her breath like a tightrope walker embarking on his most difficult stunt.

So far they had been walking at the same pace as the man on the other side of the street. It was automatic, like falling into step with a band, though he was walking fast enough to make it difficult.

What was needed was something to break the rhythm, something that would put Mad off her stride. It couldn't come from Jeanne. It was the girl herself who must unwittingly break the spell. At present she still seemed to be drawn forward by some invisible thread.

Jeanne was getting out of breath, but trying not to show it. At one moment she swallowed, making a little gurgling sound, and the contact between them had become so close during their silent walk that Mad started slightly, and turned toward her.

"Did you speak?"

"No. Why?"

"I thought you did."

That had been just enough to slow them down a little, and the man, who so far had been setting the pace, gained on them, enough for his footsteps to be no longer an obsession.

Jeanne was sure her silence was having its effect on the girl, that the latter was, so to speak, rehearsing the speech she expected her aunt to make and the answers with which she would counter it. She would have liked to get those answers off her chest. But how could she? She wasn't going to be the one to break the silence. And her aunt still said nothing.

The station reared up in front of them at the top of the street, with a few lights more brilliant than the others, and the smoke of a freight train which rose, lighter than the sky, behind the roof. There would almost certainly be a taxi there, probably two or three. Only another couple of hundred yards to go. Jeanne thought of the Fisolles hurrying up that same street at sunset, the evening before, dragging their boy after them.

For the last minute they had fallen out of step with each other. It was unimportant, but somehow Madeleine, like a soldier, instinctively felt the need to keep in step, and two or three times she slowed down to pick it up.

Even then nothing was said. Not even—as Mad must have expected—about that other departure years ago, when another girl had walked out of the creamy-white house on the other side of the bridge.

On they went. Past a streetlight. Past another, and then toward a third. Two very different steps, the one young and supple, the other that of a fat old body, who had a struggle to keep up. She managed, nonetheless, and there she was always shoulder to shoulder with the girl, relentlessly, preventing her from thinking of herself, from taking stock of the situation, from knowing what attitude to assume.

It was touch and go. The merest trifle might tilt the balance one way or the other. Jeanne was well aware of it and hardly dared breathe. She didn't pray, for she had forgotten how to, but she made an intense effort of will, as though with that alone she could force the issue.

The man on the other sidewalk had reached the station. Perhaps he was the driver of that freight train, which would soon be rambling through the dark countryside. The absence of his footsteps left a gap, making more audible those of the two women, who once again had fallen out of step.

Suddenly—heavens, what a load off Jeanne's mind!— suddenly Mad stopped, stood still for a second, then turned on her heel. And, walking back toward the streetlight they had just passed, she snarled:

"You think you've won, don't you?"

"No."

With that, they were silent again. All the way home. The people had left the terrace of the Anneau d'Or, but the woman with the bare legs was leaning out of one of the hotel

102

windows, with a man undressing behind her. The card players were still poring gravely over their game.

The bridge. Mad slowed down. Guessing why, Jeanne said
in a matter-of-fact voice:

"Désirée will help us up with the trunk."

Fortunately, Henri kept out of sight. He had stayed in the
petit salon without even turning the light on, and his sister
didn't suspect he was there listening.

"Will you give us a hand, Désirée?"

"What is it?"

"To get this trunk upstairs."

She nudged her friend to warn her to make no comment,
and the three of them managed to get it up.

"In here."

"Isn't it all right on the landing?"

"No."

It was essential that Mad should unpack then and there.
Jeanne helped her, making a point of betraying no interest in
its contents.

"There! We'd better get this thing out of your way.
Désirée and I can manage it alone, now that it's empty. You
can shut your door. Good night, Mad."

The girl hesitated, looking at the wall, then answered
tonelessly:

"Good night."

That was all.

This morning, she hadn't yet gone down. It was difficult to
face the others, however hungry she might be. She must have
been listening through her door to the sounds of people
moving about the house. She probably knew her mother was
downstairs, but had lost track of Henri. Did she know Aunt
Jeanne was confined to her room?

She would most likely have recognized Dr. Bernard's
voice, and was bound to have heard Désirée going up to the
top floor.

It was almost ten o'clock when the banister rail creaked,
and then one of the steps on which someone had stopped.

For most people there would have been nothing more to hear, but Jeanne was listening so intently that she could even hear a clock ticking in one of the rooms on the second floor.

She smoothed out the sheet, and raised her hands to tidy her discolored hair, took a deep breath, smiled, and finally called out:

"Come in."

Mad, standing in the hall, had only one step more to take.

7

"Sit down."

She waved her to the low chair that Dr. Bernard had sat on a little earlier. Something about her niece, a slight hesitation perhaps, something sensed rather than seen, made her hasten to add:

"But first of all would you mind pulling the blinds down? The light hurts my eyes."

It wasn't true, but she knew that Mad had come into the room as into a confessional, and it was better to isolate themselves from the world outside. The girl was wearing a black dress again and smelled fresh from a bath. Indeed, she was remarkably neat and trim, every hair in place. She had put no lipstick on and hardly any powder.

She looked very young like that. Quite a schoolgirl. Except that her figure was full enough to make a woman of her.

"Sit down," said Jeanne once again. Mad stood hesitantly holding the back of the chair.

They said nothing for a while, but this wasn't like their

silence the previous night. This time they were meditating, gravely, in a sort of tacit communion. Mad didn't look at her aunt, but gazed at the swollen hand that lay on the bedspread. Jeanne watched her long eyelashes blinking constantly. She knew she would look up sooner or later, and until then it was better not to say anything.

And presently she raised her face. There was no defiance in it now. Nor did she smile. All it expressed was lassitude.

"What do you think of me?" she asked in a voice that only an effort of will kept steady.

"I think, Mad, that by this time I've got a little girl in front of me who'd give heaven and earth to feel clean again."

Mad's eyes grew bigger, moistened.

"How . . . how did you know?" she just managed to stammer before grasping Jeanne's hand and bursting into tears.

There was no hurry about answering her. It wasn't time. Those tears, those hot tears that gushed out as from a spring, were too precious to be stemmed. The girl kept her face pressed against the old, swollen hand, and her sobs shook the bed. With her free hand Jeanne played dreamily with the soft brown hair.

"What," began Mad between two sobs, "what . . ."

She smiled in spite of herself at her inability to get out her words. She went on crying, but behind her tears there was something like a ray of hope in her face.

Little by little she got her breath back, though still jolted by occasional sobs.

"It's silly of me. I never cried like that in front of anyone."

She almost seemed to be asking the same question that had puzzled Dr. Bernard, as she looked hard at her aunt, whose left eye was still swollen. Others had wondered too— Louise, Henri, M. Sallenave. Even Désirée had been intrigued and had tried to pump her.

It was to all their questions, more than to only her niece's, that this old woman was smiling. A sad smile, a little mysterious. But Mad couldn't guess what it meant, for she was still of an age when people think of everything in terms of themselves.

"What made you believe in me?"

"I suppose the fact that I knew you wouldn't disappoint me."

"Nobody's ever believed in me before. Did you know that too? Everybody's mistrusted me ever since I can remember. As a little girl I was always hearing my mother say:

" 'I don't mind betting you're lying.'

"And Father. If I ever hugged him, he'd smile and ask:

" 'What's all this for? What are you trying to get out of me now?'

"With you it's been different. You said nothing, asked no questions, and made no reproaches."

"I didn't need to. You made enough reproaches to yourself, didn't you?"

"Yes. But how could you have known? Nobody could have told you that; nobody thinks me capable of remorse. In fact, no one gives me credit for any feelings at all. They think me hard, ambitious, concerned only with myself and my own pleasures. My pleasures!"

With the word, striking a false note, came a little laugh, bitter and scornful, which was painful to hear.

"I suppose Henri told you about my pleasures, my squalid pleasures. When he left me last night, he said he'd tell you everything, to make sure you'd stop me from going. I expected you to come running up to my room, bursting with indignation, to preach me a sermon. Instead of that, you said nothing. You've still said nothing.

"At least, only one thing. You understood I felt dirty. You were right. This morning I scrubbed myself violently all over. As if things like that could be removed with soap and water! It was the same every time I came back. I went straight to have a bath. It'll make you laugh, perhaps, but I'd even wash my hair, and have to spend half the night drying it."

She had got up from her chair and was pacing up and down the room. She was becoming more voluble, though the words still came out jerkily. Each time she turned around, she studied her aunt with curiosity.

"Aren't you going to ask me why I behaved like that?"

"No."

"You mean you know? Sometimes I wonder whether I know myself. Sometimes I think it was just for the sake of dragging myself through the mud."

She looked around the room with a sort of exasperation.

"This home! The life we lead here! The things we say, and the mean little thoughts behind them! . . . Was it like that in your day?"

"With this difference: that my father, whom you no doubt remember quite well, brought us up infinitely more strictly. I was never allowed out of the house alone. We weren't allowed to leave the dining room without permission, or even to speak at meals. To be one minute late for a meal was a crime. As for contradicting him, that was out of the question. If I'd come down to breakfast in my robe, or even in my slippers, I think he'd have boxed my ears. I never thought of trying. Nobody would. At half past seven in the morning I had to be properly dressed, having made my bed and done my room."

"You left," said Mad, gently, shyly, but as though that explained everything.

"At twenty-one."

"And before that?"

"I waited."

"Just waited? You didn't do anything?"

"No."

"Nothing at all?"

"Nothing at all."

"Why didn't you?"

"I don't know, Mad."

"Perhaps you had no opportunities."

"There are always opportunities for that sort of thing"

"Then it was religion."

"At sixteen I no longer believed in it."

"Or perhaps . . ."

"Yes. A matter of cleanliness. Much the same as what you were talking about just now. Also perhaps because I knew

108

that my father did it with every maid we had in the house. Once, when I dashed suddenly down to the cellars, I found him there with one of them."

"My father wasn't like that. At least I don't think so. It must have been horrible."

"Yes. I was only thirteen. It gave me a shock."

She added, smiling:

"I solemnly swore I'd never let any man do that to me. Later, I found out it could be a very beautiful thing, provided . . ."

"Provided one's in love. I've never been. I don't know that I've even wanted to love anybody. In any case, I'd never be capable of it now. Men disgust me, and sometimes, when I'm with them, I have the feeling I'm getting my revenge on them. Of course it isn't true. There's no revenge about it. I suppose it's just an excuse. You see, I ought never to have started. When I did, it was only to be like the others.

"Or, rather—not to be *like* them: to go them one better. I always wanted to do better than others, to go further. At school, up to my last year but one, I was always the top of the class in every subject. That year, for some reason or other, I was only second. After that I didn't try any more. In fact, I made a point of being one of the last."

"I was always the top myself."

"Right to the end?"

"Yes. I suppose it was vanity. I called it pride."

"Was it pride, too, that made you wait till you were twenty-one?"

"Probably."

"Yet the same thing goaded me into starting at fifteen. . . . It's funny talking to an aunt like this. I'd never have believed it possible. It was last night, just when we were getting near the station, that I began to understand. When you were in my room helping me unpack, I was on the verge of throwing myself into your arms, but I had the feeling you wouldn't want me to."

"You weren't mistaken."

"Why?"

"Because your nerves were still on edge. It was much better for you to calm down first. And, by the way, it wouldn't be a bad thing for you to run down now and get some breakfast. You can come back again afterward. You haven't had any, have you?"

"I don't need any."

"It wouldn't take you long, and you could come back at once."

"It wouldn't be the same."

"Very well. Then go to the top of the stairs and shout down to Désirée. Tell her to bring up a cup of coffee and some bread and butter. Unless you prefer a croissant. There are some."

"Do you think it would be all right?"

"Yes."

"Shall I say it's for you?"

"Yes."

"I don't like the idea of bawling at her all over the house."

"So long as it's for me, she won't mind. She knows I'm laid up."

They hardly spoke while waiting for Désirée, and in their silence was a sort of half-amused complicity.

"Perhaps I can pull the blinds up? I don't suppose the light will hurt your eyes now. Am I wrong?"

"No."

"Do you think Désirée knows about me?"

"I'm pretty sure she doesn't."

"In any case, it wouldn't matter much. There are plenty who do. Sometimes I made it plain for all to see, as though I was actually boasting about it."

They relapsed into silence again, as Désirée came up with the tray, which she put down on the bed. She seemed surprised.

"So you're hungry all of a sudden?"

Then, as a suspicion crossed her mind, she glanced at the girl.

110

"What's happening downstairs?"

"Nothing. The baby's asleep. Henri's still in the office. Madame's with the notary."

She said "Madame" on account of Mad.

"Did you call him?"

"No. He came on his own. Just a few minutes ago. He didn't ask to see you. In fact, he didn't mention you at all. He merely asked if Madame Martineau was in."

"Thank you."

"Will you want your beans for lunch just the same? It's already past eleven."

"That doesn't matter."

"You've taken your medicine?"

She went at last, and, at a glance from Jeanne, Mad pounced on the tray.

"You were ravenous—you may as well admit it."

"I was."

"Was it because of your mother you didn't want to go down?"

"Partly . . . Tell me, what ought I to do? Apologize?"

"In my opinion you'd better not refer to it at all. Just behave as if nothing has happened."

"You didn't like me for that, did you? Was it very ugly?"

"You know very well what you think of it yourself. That's all that matters."

"Everything's seething in my mind. I can't see daylight. Take what I've been saying to you this morning—I'm now beginning to wonder if it was sincere or whether I wasn't simply putting on an act. Perhaps, one day, I'll show you my diary."

"You keep a diary?"

"I used to. Chiefly *before*. It's a long time now since I wrote anything in it. But now and again, when I was particularly disgusted, I went back to it and put down just what I thought of myself. They weren't pretty thoughts. I told you . . .

"I don't really know what I told you. . . . I knew you'd

111

listen to me and would believe me, I knew you'd take an interest in me. In fact, I knew it right from the start, and I wanted to intrigue you. Perhaps it was for the sake of talking to you as I'm doing now that I came back last night. I wanted to prove to you that I was worth taking an interest in, and I was determined to come up to your expectations. I'm telling you the truth now, Aunt Jeanne.

"I'm a filthy creature. Vicious through and through.

"When you spoke just now of your father in the cellars, I bent my head down so you wouldn't see me blush. Because in my case it was just the opposite. I used to creep out of bed at night and peep through the keyhole of my parents' room in the hope of seeing something."

"Did you?"

"No. They always had the light out. But I used to listen and try and guess what they were doing. And then, back in my own bed, I'd . . ."

"Yes, yes, I know."

"You too?"

Her aunt merely nodded. Then she added:

"How old were you then?"

"Thirteen. . . . Did girls at your school talk dirty, the way they do nowadays?"

"Some."

"And draw dirty pictures?"

"Probably."

"At fourteen I knew every bad word in the language. And what they meant too. While at home they thought me an innocent child. It used to make me furious to see my brothers whispering together, then burst out laughing. They'd never tell me what they were laughing at.

"Of course Julien was away a lot, in Poitiers, at the university. I didn't see a lot of him. And when he was home he didn't think me old enough to be worth taking any notice of. He never realized I was growing up. With Henri it was different. There's only a couple of years between us, and I made him open up."

"And made him take you along with him?"

"Yes. That's how it all began. Not that it made any difference. If it hadn't been for Henri, I'd have carried on just the same. I might have started a bit later—that's all."

And looking gravely at her aunt, she added:

"You see, I'm thoroughly vicious, as I said. It's in my blood, and there's nothing to be done about it."

Then, working herself up:

"It isn't the thing in itself. . . . You know what I mean. . . . Most of the time I don't even get any pleasure out of it. And I know beforehand that I'll be disgusted afterward."

"Yet you do it just the same."

"Yes. That's what I mean by being vicious. I do it so as not to stay at home, for the sake of a ride in a car. I'd do it, if only for the pleasure of showing off before my friends, driving through town with a man beside me. An open car preferably. Clever, isn't it? And to sit on a café terrace like that creature we saw last night. Oh, yes. I've been just like that. That's what made me so ashamed. It looks so stupid when others do it. And so revolting.

"Above all, stupid. Just to make yourself interesting, to excite men, and make them say a lot of silly things with a nervous giggle, get them to take you to the beaches, casinos, and dance halls, and buy you cocktails. After which, they kiss you, breathing noisily, their breath stinking of alcohol, and in the end, trembling like dogs when they get up on their hind legs, they upend you in some shoddy little hotel room, if it isn't by the roadside or on the back seat of the car.

"Why have I gone through with it all this time? Tell me that, Aunt Jeanne."

Perhaps, after all, she would rather have had the blinds down now, to shut out the sunny streets and shops, the Anneau d'Or with its terrace, where vacationers were sitting in the shade over their *apéritifs*.

"Sometimes, when I come back, I feel I can't touch myself till I've scrubbed my hands with pumice stone, and when I lie in bed at night I can't get rid of the vile taste of wet kisses.

113

For a long time I went on going to confession, sometimes immediately after. And then one day the priest asked me whether I didn't get a sensual pleasure out of telling him all my sins. I had to admit he was right. Not that it was sensual; it was just one more way of trying to make myself interesting. I think I even tried to see his face sometimes to find out whether he was shocked.

"Well? Don't you think I'm vicious?

"I spend the whole week moping around the house trying to find something to interest myself in. I think if I was really good at something or other, painting or playing the piano, for instance, I'd drop the rest altogether.

"But I'm only average at everything I do, even swimming and tennis. So when Friday comes around, I start calling people up. There's one fellow I met at Royan, a married man with three children—I've only to lift a finger and he'll come darting here all the way from Paris. He's the one I was out with on Sunday. . . . What did you say?"

"I didn't say anything."

Possibly her lips had moved a little, as she had muttered to herself:

"Poor child!"

"It's pretty hopeless, isn't it? You must admit it's a lot worse than you ever imagined. There's another thing. I may as well tell you all, though this is something I couldn't even tell to a priest. It makes me feel ill even to think of it. Sometimes I . . . No, don't look at me. It's terribly hard to say. . . . Sometimes I even arranged for another man to look on. I liked to see him getting all worked up. I wanted him to admire me, to desire me wildly, and to think me the only girl in the world capable of . . ."

The tears flowed again, but not in the same way this time. She wept without sobs, without troubling to hide her face, unconcerned at being seen with her features all puckered.

She simply let them flow, right down her cheeks, past the corners of her mouth, to quiver for a moment on the point of her chin, while she went on in a voice that resembled her mother's when she was in one of her fits:

"How can you expect me ever to be decent again, to have a man of my own who'd treat me as a real woman and give me children? I don't even know whether I could have any.

"Not very long ago I went to a doctor. Not Dr. Bernard, but one in another town. He refused to have anything to do with me, and I had, after dark, to slink into a filthy hovel where an old woman did for me what you can guess. Nobody knew. And the following night, to make sure no one heard, I put a pillow over my face—in case I cried out. I might have died like that, all alone in my own room. . . . Then there was all the money I had to find, by hook or by crook, to pay the old woman.

"Since then, my insides have never been quite right again. I get pains. And yet, month after month, I go on just the same. Do you understand that—you who seem to understand everything?

"The men notice nothing. They're too pleased with themselves, too busy having a good time. If they only knew what I thought of them! If they only knew how I hated them! Particularly when they come close and look into my eyes with that awful expression on their faces.

"I'm reduced to utter misery, Aunt Jeanne. That's true at any rate, even if, for the rest, I sometimes wander from the truth and touch it up a bit. It really is. You must believe me. I beg you to believe me.

"And it's true too—what you said just now—that I'd give anything to feel clean again. And I'd stay clean. I'm seventeen, Aunt Jeanne. Seventeen last month. And to think that at that age I'm already a . . ."

"You're a woman, Mad."

The words came as a slight shock, and Mad was suddenly brought to a standstill, looking at her aunt incredulously, with a frown on her forehead. She thought for a moment, making an effort to understand, then asked almost challengingly:

"What do you mean by that?"

"Just what I say—no more, no less. Your brother's a man. Your father and grandfather were men, and no more than men. Your mother's a woman. So are you; and so is Alice."

"Alice! She can do whatever comes into her head without feeling a pang of shame."

"What do you know about it?"

"The very first time it happened to her, she hooked a husband."

"He's dead now."

"That doesn't alter the fact that she fell on her feet, all right. She's a married woman."

"What do you know about it?"

"You keep on saying that. What I know is that most people go through life ignoring all the problems. They may not always be happy, but at least they're quite satisfied with themselves."

"And once more I say: What do you know about it?"

At that, Mad lost patience, bursting out:

"I suppose you're going to tell me you too are disgusted with yourself?"

"Me too."

"Why?"

"For a lot of reasons. For a whole life, which would make too long a story to tell you now, though I'll tell it to you one day if you still want me to. Today I'll merely tell you the last chapter, which is quite recent history.

"On Sunday morning a fat old woman with a round, pasty face knocked at the door of this house, and, because it was Aunt Jeanne, no one stopped to ask himself what she was doing here."

"That's true."

"Well, your Aunt Jeanne had crept here piteously, looking for somewhere to lay her head, because she had sunk so low, because she was so jaded and so nauseated with herself that all she wanted was a bit of shelter where she could wait for the end.

"It was her last chance. She came from far away, and was so worn out she hardly dared hope to reach her destination.

"At Poitiers, where she changed, Jeanne—yes, your Aunt

116

Jeanne—had to have a couple of stiff brandies in the refreshment room to bolster her courage—at least that was her excuse—taking cover in a corner because she was afraid of being recognized."

"Like Mother."

"And the same evening, in the hotel over the way, she had to have another and still another, and if she didn't get here earlier on Sunday it was because she had a hangover."

The bluntness of the expression made the girl sit up.

"In Paris, where she stopped for a night on the way, Aunt Jeanne found herself in a sordid little bar, where, jostling with men, she had drink after drink served in thick grubby glasses. Before that, at Istanbul . . ."

"Aunt Jeanne!"

"You've got to hear this, Mad, though you can keep it to yourself. At Istanbul, Aunt Jeanne, who'd already worked as a servant . . ."

"Like Désirée . . ."

"At Istanbul she sank to the lowest trade of all, the absolutely lowest, the one that men themselves despise, and for which they employ their harshest expressions, the trade for which, in most countries, you're put in prison."

"You . . ."

She hadn't understood and looked incredulously at her aunt's flabby face and shapeless body.

"No. It's not what you think. I was the one to receive the customers, smiling all over my face, asking them their preferences in words that left nothing to the imagination, after which I'd clap my hands like a schoolmistress, summoning a troop of scantily dressed girls, who'd stand in a row, while the men prodded them as if they were cattle in the market."

Madeleine hung her head. She had nothing more to say now. Neither did Jeanne say anything for a while, as she gazed at a slate-colored pigeon that had landed on the windowsill.

"Have you understood now?"

Mad nodded.

117

"What have you understood?"

"I don't know. Everything."

"Can you still look at me?"

Mad looked up. But only after a moment's hesitation. Her eyes were grave and troubled.

"You see! You couldn't shed tears on my hand now, as you did a little while ago. But I think it's better this way."

"Yes, you're right," said Mad, swallowing with an effort.

She was visibly wanting to escape now, to get away from this room in which they'd been boxed up together long enough and had laid bare too many secrets.

"You can go now. I hope Monsieur Bigeois hasn't gone yet. Tell your mother I'd like to see him. She can come up too."

"Yes, Aunt Jeanne."

"On your way down, bathe your eyes with cold water and powder yourself. And pass me that bottle of eau de Cologne, will you?"

Mad got it from the chest of drawers that had been there in the same place forty years ago, when Jeanne was Mad's age. Jeanne couldn't help saying:

"That was my chest of drawers when I was a girl. This was my room. . . . Now, run along."

"Thanks."

She may have been anxious to get away, but that didn't make it easy to go. In fact, it was almost as difficult as coming. For a moment she stood in the middle of the room, her arms hanging by her sides, then walked stiffly toward the door. Halfway there, she suddenly made up her mind, swung around, and walked up to the bed, where she bent down and kissed Jeanne's forehead, which now smelled of eau de Cologne.

Referring to the scent, Jeanne almost said:

"You see, I want to make myself clean too."

But it would have struck a false note. Silence was better, and it was broken only by the sound of Mad's retreating steps, which were at first quite sedate. Only when she was halfway down the stairs did she break into a run, romping down the rest of the way like any stripling.

She didn't stop to bathe her eyes; then Jeanne heard her scampering down again and calling out as she opened the door of the *petit salon:*

"Mother! Aunt Jeanne wants . . ."

The rest was inaudible as the door closed behind her.

So now there was only this fat old Jaja, all swollen up in her bed, including her left eye, which looked as though it had received a punch, making her like some old drunk past whom parents hastily drag their children, telling them not to look around.

Her lips were dry, as was her throat. Mechanically, her hand went up to her breast and pressed on the soft warm flesh over her heart, as it had in the train. She thought of that little cupboard in the bathroom, where Louise kept her secret hoard. Could she get around Désirée and persuade her to . . .

Then she slipped down under the covers and, forgetting all about Monsieur Bigeois, shut her eyes. Tired out, her lips quivered as they framed a word that was, however, inaudible.

"Clean . . ."

8

He went up with a slow but precise step, stopping at every third or fourth stair, though not with the taut, anxious look on his face of someone suffering from heart trouble. Nor was he short of breath. He was just a man who measured his strength and avoided all superfluous effort. And each time he stopped, he calmly looked at the wall or the stairs rising in front of him.

Louise, looking smaller than ever, followed him, surprised and embarrassed at each pause, and feeling she ought to fill it in with conversation.

"I'm afraid they're steep, these stairs," she muttered apologetically.

He didn't turn around, didn't even answer. His back answered for him, proclaiming his contempt for all commonplace or useless remarks.

She tried once again:

"If I'd known that my sister-in-law was going to be ill, I'd have put her in one of the second-floor rooms. She was the one who suggested going into her old room at the top."

Again no answer. At this rate, when were they ever going to get to the third floor?

What age would he be, this M. Bigeois? Jeanne had at first assumed he must be the son of the notary she had known, whom even as a girl she had regarded as quite an old man. He must have been close to ninety now, if he wasn't more. But he still held himself straight as a poker. His complexion was pink as a baby's, looking a little artificial under a shock of white hair brushed straight up.

"Can I bring Monsieur Bigeois in, Jeanne?"

"Yes. Come in."

He came in with the same detached expression on his face, the same aloofness to his surroundings, as if he were inspecting a house for sale. Only after a moment did he turn on Jeanne a look of professional curiosity. He made it so obvious, that his lack of politeness seemed quite intentional. He seemed to have no use for civilities, except for the bare minimum that was practically unavoidable. Instead of saying good morning and asking after her health in the usual vague phrases, he merely uttered a single word, and he uttered it, in all probability, with that diabolical pleasure that the old sometimes take in the spectacle of younger people on a sickbed.

"Dropsy?"

She remembered him as a terrifying person when she was a little girl, and it was almost with the timidity of a little girl that she answered:

"It's nothing serious. A few days' rest, and I'll be up and about again."

"That's what they all say."

"I've had it before."

She noticed that Louise looked worried, not nerve-racked and hysterical, as she had been on other occasions, but like someone who is suddenly faced with grave and precise problems.

"Monsieur Bigeois didn't want to come up, but I per-

121

suaded him to come and tell you what he's just told me."

"Sit down, won't you, Monsieur Bigeois?"

But he didn't like the look of the low chair by the bed, to which she pointed. He removed it and fetched another, which was standing against the wall. Before sitting down, he examined it critically, as though valuing it or making sure it would bear his weight.

"I take it you saw the notice I put in the papers," he said.

And, without waiting for an answer, he went on:

"For reasons of your own, which I know very well, you allowed your death to be assumed. You snapped your fingers at your inheritance, thinking you'd never return. Yet here you are, just the same."

"It wasn't for that I came back," she protested. "And if I asked you to come up and see me this morning . . ."

She wanted to explain, both to him and to Louise, that her intention was nothing less than to renounce any claim she might legally have on the estate. But he cut her short.

"As things are at present, it makes very little difference what you intended to do or not to do."

There was probably nobody who knew as well as he did the families of the district and their secrets. And it wasn't merely the families; he knew every stone of which the town was built.

For what was he trying to get his own back by adopting that icy tone, behind which it was obvious he was smacking his lips over their misfortunes?

Perhaps Louise was sorry for Jeanne, who with her swollen face and bruised eye indeed cut a pitiful figure, because she quickly intervened with:

"Monsieur Bigeois has brought bad news."

"I'm not surprised. From what Monsieur Sallenave told me . . ."

The lawyer shrugged his shoulders contemptuously.

"Sallenave's only a clerk. There are things he doesn't know."

Jeanne was taken aback.

122

referring to the Fisolles' claim?" she asked.

solles don't matter a scrap one way or the other. Fisolle called me up this morning, asking for an immediate valuation of the estate. I told him it wouldn't take five minutes!"

"Things are much worse than you think, Jeanne."

Louise was calmer and more self-controlled than her sister-in-law had yet seen her. She was obviously stunned, but was not merely drifting.

"We shall have to sell."

"Everything? Even the house?"

"Yes," put in the old man, "everything—the house and all its contents, the stock and good will of the business. And when that's done there'll still be a deficit large enough to have made things very awkward indeed for Robert Martineau, had he been alive. It's not for me to sit in judgment on him. It's many a long year since I expected anything of human beings. Knowing them as I do, I had a pretty shrewd idea, when he left me on Saturday, how he would decide to meet the situation."

"You think that was the easy way out?"

He didn't deign to answer that question. The look he gave the fat woman lying in front of him was answer enough. He coughed and took out his handkerchief. Then, as though the words had a meaning for him alone, he observed:

"I knew his grandfather. I knew his father. I knew him and his brothers. I know his children."

"Why did he come to see you?"

"Why do people come to see me on a Saturday evening after office hours?"

She wondered whether downstairs he had been more human and tried to soften the blow when he broke the news to Louise. He had certainly had time enough. It had been quite a long interview. Probably he regarded it as an unwarranted imposition that he was being made to go over the ground a second time, and was determined to punish Jeanne for being the cause of it.

"I knew my brother needed money to pay some bills o
Monday morning, and that there was nothing in the till. Not
a centime."

"But on Monday Monsieur Sallenave gave me some," ex-
claimed Louise.

Then she suddenly understood and looked at her sister-in-
law with embarrassment.

"When people speak of needing money," said the lawyer,
"they are generally referring to needs that can, at a pinch, be
satisfied. Beyond a certain point, when the need gets out of
all proportion to the security that can be offered, it's another
matter altogether. You can call it what you like. That clerk of
yours, Sallenave, worries over the little bills that have to be
paid and gets as frightened as a child. He is a child, for that
matter. I can remember his grandfather going from door to
door with a cart of vegetables. You have returned at a very
inappropriate moment, Mademoiselle Martineau, and you
would no doubt have done much better to have stayed where
you were."

Mademoiselle! He didn't call her Madame Lauer, knowing very well she had never been married. Jeanne recalled
the fact that an aunt of François Lauer's had been both a
client and a friend of his.

"I thought I might as well wait till after the funeral. Now
it's my plain duty to inform you of the situation. In fact, I did
so downstairs, and I have no idea why Madame Martineau
should have wanted me to repeat what I told her."

"What did Robert say to you on Saturday?"

"What everybody says under those circumstances. He was
a beaten man. He couldn't see any way out. There wasn't a
way out. But he still went on blindly groping for one, and he
seemed to think, because I was his lawyer—still more because
I had been his father's—that I could work a miracle."

"How much did he need?"

"A few million francs. Realizing all his assets at the high-
est possible price, we might with luck meet half the claims.
That's why I told Monsieur Fisolle just now that for all prac-

tical purposes the valuation of the estate was as good as done. The heirs' only course is to renounce any benefits under his will, or they'll find themselves saddled with debts that it will take them the rest of their lives to pay off."

"How did he get in this mess?"

"I was waiting for that question. Your sister-in-law asked me the same thing. It's what everyone wants to know. People live in the same house, sleep in the same bed or in neighboring rooms, sit down for meals together three times a day, and then are surprised to discover, one fine day, that they know nothing whatever about each other."

"You forget I left Pont Saint-Jean thirty-six years ago."

"I don't forget it for a moment. It was I who advised your father to take no steps to trace you—though, considering his character, I don't think he needed that advice. And I was quite sure, when I published that notice, which I was legally obliged to publish, that it would meet with no response."

"Did you know where I was?"

He stared at her without answering, with a look that seemed to come from another world, hard, icy, merciless.

With an air of resignation he waited for further questions, pulling a large watch out of his waistcoat pocket and winding it up.

"You have nothing in particular to say to me?" asked Jeanne.

That seemed to surprise him.

"Why should I? I've said all I have to say to Robert's widow."

"You might have gone about it a bit more gently."

That was an outrageous thing to say, and he put Jeanne in her place with a glare that made her redden.

"I'm sorry. . . . And I'm sorry to have made you climb up all these stairs. I've arrived here to find a family crisis, and I'm doing my best to . . ."

"Family crisis!" he snorted contemptuously. "The whole thing's quite simple. There are families that rise and others that go to the wall. Now that young couple opposite, who

125

have taken over the Anneau d'Or, are on the rise. The fellow was a waiter in a café, and his wife's the daughter of poor Italians. In ten years they'll have bought up two or three houses in town or farms in the country. If it hadn't cropped up so soon, they'd doubtless have been candidates for this house, to make it into an annex of the hotel."

This was obviously a subject to his taste. There was no need to drag the words out of him now.

"Your grandfather—there was a man on the upgrade too."

There were two photographs of him in the family album. In one of them he was shown in a jacket with brass buttons and leather gaiters, holding a gun in his hand. A dog lay at his feet. With his fierce, pointed mustache, he looked like a poacher ready to shoot down any gendarme who got in his way.

It was he who had been the landlord of the Anneau d'Or in the days when it was Pont Saint-Jean's only inn, the stopping place for teamsters' carts. There was no stone bridge then, only a wooden one, and the river hadn't yet been walled with stone embankments. He could neither read nor write. There wasn't any slaughterhouse in those days either, and it was in the shed behind the hotel that cattle were killed, the hides being washed in the river.

In that photograph, done on a thin sheet of bronzed metal, he was a man of forty. In the other he was an old man, his finely lined face flanked by white whiskers, but his features were still somewhat forbidding and he was obviously jealous of his dignity.

At that time, he had already bought the land on which the present house stood, and had built the first cellars.

His son, Jeanne's father, had concentrated on the wine business, getting rid of the hotel, which, in other hands, had blossomed into what it now was.

Louis was a big, strong man with a florid face, a hard drinker, though never drunk. His wife had died giving birth to Robert, after which the widower had consoled himself with the servants.

"So was your father on the upgrade," pursued the lawyer

126

in his cold, detached voice. "And I have no doubt the family would still have been rising if your two eldest brothers had not been killed in the first war."

He had the history of the family at his fingertips and he wasn't going to miss the opportunity of showing it.

"But Robert was the only one left. He did his best, and scraped along. For a time, thanks to certain circumstances, he did very well indeed, and he made the mistake of thinking it was now his turn to launch out. It's the same thing over and over again. I could give you fifty cases in this neighborhood, and I wouldn't have to go far afield. . . . There was just one chance left, his son Julien. Of course one can't say anything for certain, but he might well have done something. He was ambitious."

He put a white pill on his tongue. Then he took out his handkerchief, blew his nose vigorously, and inspected the result with interest.

"Your sister-in-law asked my advice about the future of the remaining children, and I gave her some. I don't think the family can very well go on living in this town after their house and property have been sold. Henri's failed twice in his final exams and can't try a third time. Since he's not trained for anything in particular and would probably think it beneath his dignity to work as a farm laborer, he'll inevitably end up in an office. At Poitiers, for instance, or some other big town.

"I imagine his mother would wish to go with him, and, in view of the fact that there's no one else to support her, she can't very well do otherwise. Madeleine could earn something too. She could get a job in a shop or take up manicuring.

"As for you, you've managed to keep afloat so far and will no doubt continue to.

"That leaves the other one."

It was only then that it occurred to Jeanne that the old man's ferocity might not be pure sadism. There was perhaps a reason for it, perhaps even a justification.

"Which other one? You mean Alice?"

She looked at Louise, who turned her head away. She already knew.

"No. Not Alice—the mother of the other child," he answered, pleased with the effect he was producing. "For some time before his death your brother was carrying on with another woman, whom he kept in a suburb of Poitiers. Unfortunately for her, he didn't buy her a house, but merely rented one."

"Who is she?"

"If I told you her name, it wouldn't mean anything to you. She doesn't come from these parts. A commonplace little thing, of humble parentage, who was working in a glove shop in the town."

"Young?"

"Twenty-two."

Turning to her sister-in-law, Jeanne asked:

"Did Robert go to see her often?"

"Each time he pretended to be traveling on business."

"Did you know?"

"One day I found a baby's rattle in his coat pocket. I thought it was for Bob, and that he'd forgotten about it. Later I found a prescription from a children's doctor in Poitiers, a man we didn't know."

"Did you speak to him about it?"

"Yes. It's an old story."

Louise glanced at the lawyer, then gave Jeanne a meaningful look, begging her not to pursue the subject in front of him.

"How old is the child, Monsieur Bigeois?"

"Two. He's called Lucien, after his mother, whose name is Lucienne. But don't get the idea that it was keeping them that ruined him financially. Of the two establishments, it wasn't that one that swallowed up the money. A little three-room house run on very modest lines. Besides, when he met the girl, his affairs were already in a bad way. In fact, it was probably because he was living in fear and insecurity that he longed for a little haven of peace."

"I think I understand."

He made a gesture to indicate that it didn't make the slightest difference whether this fat creature who had come back into their midst understood her brother's perplexities or not.

"Your sister-in-law asked me just now how he could leave his family in such a desperate plight. I suppose you'll ask me the same question."

"No."

"I would have answered by asking you in turn who, among those around him, had ever lifted a finger to give him help or support."

"I know."

"This other woman has never made any demands on him."

"Has she kept her job?"

"Your brother didn't want her to. First of all because of the baby. Secondly because, when he went to see her, it was generally on the spur of the moment, at any time of day. It was chiefly about her that he spoke to me on Saturday evening."

Louise said nothing. With her chin in her hand, she gazed at the foot of the bed.

"Unfortunately, I am unable to do any more for her and her child than I can for the rest of you. Already on Tuesday, the day after I called on her . . ."

"You went to see her on Monday?"

She began to wonder whether she was discovering another side of this man.

"Who else would have brought her the news?"

"Did my brother ask you to?"

"He begged me, if anything should happen to him, to go and break the news to her in such a way that she wouldn't think too badly of him. As I was saying, on Tuesday she had already started looking for work, and she called me up in the evening to say she'd found something. As for where all your brother's money went to—and other people's money too, for that matter—it's a long story, and I see no point in repeating in detail the explanation I gave Madame Martineau. Suffice it to say that instead of confining himself to his normal business as a wine merchant, he started speculating, thinking that was the only way he could get himself out of the mess he had got into over his income tax. He made a lot of purchases on credit, if you know what that means. Wine in bulk. Whole shiploads of it, or practically. It's this side of the affair that your little Sallenave, in his innocence, doesn't even suspect, because these transactions never passed through the books of the business. For them Robert dealt directly with a broker in Poitiers.

"Last month the Chamber of Deputies passed a new law controlling the sale of wine, and, from one day to the next, prices collapsed. That was the last straw. Admittedly, the crash would have come sooner or later, but it might have been held off for months or even years.

"It's tomorrow that his creditors are due to attach all his property. He knew that on Saturday. As you see, there weren't many solutions open to him. Two, in my opinion. Three, if you like, but he didn't even consider the third."

"Which was?"

"To stand his ground and face the music, which would probably have meant going to prison."

"And the other two?"

"He chose one of them."

"That leaves the one he rejected."

"Yes. And until young Bernard called up just before lunch on Sunday morning . . ."

"Dr. Bernard called you up?"

"I had already warned him."

"Of what was going to happen?"

"Of what might happen. For a long time Bernard has known all about your brother. He was his doctor. He even went over to Poitiers, at Robert's request, to examine the newborn baby. Your brother was frightened of some hereditary disease. He also had the idea he might be too old."

"So Dr. Bernard knew!" she mused.

Perhaps he had stayed in on purpose that morning to be ready when he was wanted.

She came back to the subject they were discussing.

"The last solution?"

"I thought he might get out of the country, taking this woman and the child with him, and start over again somewhere else. That was really the only sort of life open to him."

She felt she was beginning to understand, though it wasn't yet very clear. Her mind worked in images, and these were still rather incoherent. She hadn't had time to sort them out.

Once upon a time, there had stood, where the red brick Anneau d'Or was now, a humble inn for teamsters and their like, with a wooden shed behind, on the bank of the river, where twice a week animals were brought for slaughtering.

Later, on the other side of the bridge, a creamy-white house had risen up against the blue sky, this house built by her father, which she had known as a child.

But, inside, that house had seemed both to her and to her young brother more like a prison, oppressive and forever unchangeable.

She had fled. Robert had stayed. And those rooms never changed, neither did the boy, who at forty still trembled before his father. He had married, married "that Taillefer girl," daughter of an eccentric doctor who interested himself in everything except his patients. And if she was tolerated, she was nonetheless looked down on.

Then the war, just after Louis Martineau's death. Easy money. The chance at last to change the unchangeable, to step out of the rut, to begin to live . . .

"Poor Robert," she muttered.

"Yes," said the notary, agreeing with her for once. "He hadn't the courage."

He didn't explain what he meant by that. Did he mean the courage to break away and start over, shaking off all the responsibilities, the cares, the resentments that had accumulated with the years till they formed a burden that he no longer had the strength to carry?

M. Bigeois had looked at Louise as he spoke, and Jeanne

131

recalled the scene the latter had made on Sunday, the sequel, no doubt, of countless others. Then her mind wandered on to Henri telephoning from some village in Normandy, Madeleine coming in in wet shorts and blouse and hiding away upstairs, and Alice, with her nerves stretched to breaking point, almost ready to batter her baby's head against the wall.

"I suppose," she said, "Louise can count on no money at all?"

"None whatever. She has the right to remove her personal effects, one bed per person, and possibly a table and a few chairs. No more."

"When?"

"No one can confiscate without permission from the court. That will be given tomorrow morning. The sheriff's representative will come around the following day to seal everything up. I shall be here. Considering Henri's age, there won't be any question of appointing a guardian for him. But, at seventeen, Mad will have to have one. Madame Martineau can tell you about that, however; we went into it thoroughly downstairs."

He got up and bowed toward the bed. When he raised his head, Jeanne caught a little glint in his eye, no doubt of irony. "I trust you will soon be well again."

"I'll come down with you," said Louise.

"Thank you, though I daresay I know this house almost as well as you do."

"I'll be back in a moment, Jeanne."

"All right."

It was Désirée, however, who came up first, bringing a dish of French beans.

"So you're moving, are you?"

"Who said so?"

"I heard some scraps of their conversation downstairs. Enough to tell me there wasn't much chance of my getting my wages."

"I'm sorry about that. I had no idea things were in that state."

"It doesn't matter. And anyway I wouldn't blame you. The only thing is—I'll have to find another job. They won't take me back at the Anneau d'Or now that the season's nearly over. And the same goes for all the other hotels around here. It's a pity; I much prefer hotels to private service."

She listened at the door.

"Here's your sister-in-law coming up. I'll leave you. How's this business going to affect you? I suppose you've got a bit of money laid by. . . . But I'll come back presently."

As she went she couldn't help having another dig at Jeanne.

"And you who wanted us to spend half the night cleaning up the house as though for a wedding! And this morning urged me to be on my best behavior!"

She laughed, though with a touch of resentment. Louise passed her on the stairs. When she came in, she sat down on the chair M. Bigeois had vacated and looked at Jeanne in silence. She had got past the moment of anxiety and agitation. At this point, most questions seemed to answer themselves.

Yes, everything was simplified, drawn clearly in black and white in lines the old notary had traced with blithe ferocity.

"Have the children been told?"

"Not yet. Henri's just come in from the office. He was worried about some order. Thought they oughtn't to deliver the stuff, and asked when lunch would be, because Monsieur Sallenave wants him back in the office at two."

"And Mad?"

"She's playing with the baby. I can't think what you've done to her. I haven't seen her so happy for ages. She insisted on giving Bob his bottle. What did the doctor say about you?"

"Of course . . . I was almost forgetting I was ill. I suppose, because I'm not one of Robert's family, I won't be entitled to take a bed with me!"

"Can you really joke about it?"

"I'm sorry. I didn't mean it. But, you see, I'd got myself so worked up about everything."

"About us?"

"About you. About myself. About all sorts of things. I don't know why I should have jumped to the conclusion, as soon as I came into the house, that I had a part to play here."

"You had. And you played it."

Did Louise realize what infinite pains Jeanne had taken ever since Sunday to keep the peace and, that morning, to have everything arranged so that each of them would see his surroundings with fresh eyes?

"I began to play it, and I took myself very seriously. For me the pivot of everything was the house itself. I felt that, so long as the walls were standing, so long as everything was in its place and life went on smoothly from day to day, the fates would be placated. It was silly, and I don't suppose it would have worked. I seemed to forget that it was to escape this very house that I fled years ago."

"And Robert? Do you also think it was because of . . ."

"What did he say to you?"

"When?"

"When you spoke to him about the baby's prescription."

"He began by lying. He tried to make out it was just an accident, a passing adventure that had tripped him, that he wasn't even sure he was the father, but that, since it was possible, he was bound to do his duty."

"Did you believe him?"

"Yes. I couldn't even imagine the possibility of its being otherwise. But I asked him to keep away from Poitiers and to send the girl her money by mail. And I kept an eye on him. Then, when he felt he was cornered, he blurted out the truth."

"He admitted he loved her?"

"Yes. If only that had been all! But, once he started, it flowed out in torrents. A flood of hatred that he'd been bottling up for years. He told me that he had never loved me, never, that he had married me because his father thought it was high time to have a woman in the house, and that he had picked me to get back at the old man, knowing I was just the kind of girl he couldn't stand."

"Didn't he refer to the children?"

"Yes. But by that time I wasn't listening. It was too horrible. I felt I'd go mad. He made me believe he had always hated the sight of me and had always held me to be responsible for everything that went wrong."

"When did it take place, this scene?"

"Three months ago. That was the first time. There were others after."

"But you carried on just as before?"

"What else could I do?"

"Admittedly . . ." murmured Jeanne, studying her sister-in-law.

"I got him to promise that he'd never walk out on us."

"He promised that?"

"He swore he wouldn't."

"Why?"

"For the sake of the children."

"And the other?"

"What other?"

"The other child?"

"It's not my fault if he had a child by that woman. You're looking at me all of a sudden as Robert did lately. As for Monsieur Bigeois, he was scarcely polite, and seemed delighted to be bringing me bad news. Was I Robert's wife or wasn't I?"

"Well, if you put it that way . . ."

"Am I the mother of his children?"

"Of course, Louise. Of course. Don't let's argue about it. I really don't know why we're talking about it at all."

"But you judge me pretty severely, don't you?"

"What for?"

"For everything, for what you've found out about me, for Henri and Mad and their goings-on. I know you think it's all my fault."

"What are you going to do?"

"I don't see there's anything I can do except what the lawyer says. Have you any ideas? But I don't know where we're going to find the money even to pay our fares to another town. I suppose I've a right to sell my jewelry, but I've got precious little. If worse comes to worst, I could go to my cousin. I guess she'd lend me a few thousand francs at the price of a long sermon and making me sign a lot of papers. You know her. The one that came to the funeral yesterday. She's as rich as she's close-fisted."

"When are you going to break the news to Henri and Mad?"

"I don't know. As a matter of fact, I was thinking of asking you to do it. You've got more influence over them than I have. This morning Henri was almost polite to me, and I can only think it was your doing. As for Mad, she's another person since she came down after seeing you. What bothers me is Désirée. I don't know what to do about her."

"Don't worry. She doesn't expect to get paid. She'll be leaving as soon as she can get another job."

"And you? What are you going to do?"

"You heard what Monsieur Bigeois said about that. Keep my head above water somehow, as I've done hitherto."

"But where? Why not stay with us?"

That was what she had been leading up to, and she pretended not to be anxious as she waited for Jeanne's answer.

"It'll be another mouth to feed out of what the children can earn."

"I mean to work too."

"What kind of work?"

"I don't know. Lady's companion, perhaps. Or I could sit at a cash desk. Anything. Then you could keep house for us."

"What about my poor old legs?"

"You say yourself they'll be all right in a few days."

"Suppose it came on again?"

"We'd look after you."

"I'll think it over. I promise I will, Louise. As a matter of fact, I'd thought of it already. It's incredible the amount of thinking I've done since I woke up this morning."

"You're talking like Mad now."

"What do you mean?"

"Like Mad when she came downstairs this morning. She seemed suddenly to have shaken off all her cares and to be quite lighthearted. She didn't say much, but what she did she said playfully, as though nothing mattered any longer. It's the same with you. You take it all quite casually, and even joke about it."

"I'm not joking, Louise. Only, for me too, there aren't a lot of alternatives to choose from. And I don't suppose it'll be very long now before there'll be only one, which I must take whether I like it or not."

Her face clouded, for this question of choice reminded her of the notary's three possible solutions, of the one her brother had chosen, still more of the one he had turned his back on.

"Go and have your lunch now. The children must be waiting. Send them up to me presently."

"Both together?"

Jeanne thought for a moment.

"Why not? At this stage . . ."

It was no longer necessary to put on kid gloves.

9

When Dr. Bernard arrived at half past eight the next morning, he had to come in through the courtyard and kitchen, because the house was in such a turmoil that no one heard the bell. It was like the last-minute scurry before going off on a vacation. All the windows were open, as though that alone had a symbolic meaning. Doors kept slamming and drafts swept through the house, blowing papers around. Trunks and suitcases lay everywhere, in the rooms and on the landings. No respect was shown to carpets, and voices echoed as though the house was already empty. Even Louise, still in her robe and slippers, had been infected by the fever and was joining in the joyous holocaust.

For two hoots they would literally have smashed up the place. Gleefully.

It had begun the previous afternoon, immediately after Jeanne had broken the news to her nephew and niece. Even at that fateful moment the conversation was tinged with gaiety, or at any rate with relief. Louise had been quite wrong to be afraid of telling them. But then, she was ready to take fright at anything. Jeanne knew beforehand that the prospect of a change, whatever it might be, would be welcomed as a blessing, if not a deliverance.

"The house is going to be sold," she announced, eying them keenly.

"Where are we going to live?"

It was Mad whose first reaction was to ask:

"Are you coming with us?"

Not necessarily that she wanted it. Now that she had laid herself bare, she might even rather dread the idea of having a witness permanently at her side.

"I don't know yet."

"When are we going?"

"As soon as possible. Probably tomorrow. It depends on what success your mother has this afternoon."

For Louise, in deep mourning, had gone off to see her old cousin, who lived just outside town.

"Are we never coming back here?"

"No."

"Are we going to Paris?"

"Paris or Poitiers. Monsieur Bigeois brought bad news this morning. You're ruined."

"Ah!"

What does the word "ruin" mean to people of that age?

"Everything's got to be sold, except your personal belongings."

"The car too?"

"The car too."

"How are we going to get there?"

"By train, no doubt."

They listened with only moderate interest as she explained what attachment meant. As soon as Henri realized they had no more money, he burst out:

"I'll go to work."

"Your mother's counting on you, and on Mad too."

"I'll get a job as a reporter. Can we start packing?"

That was what really interested them. To pack. To cut the strings. To be off. They were impatient to begin a new life to obliterate the old one. That's why they wouldn't have minded wrecking the house.

"Will you help me down with the trunks, Mad?"

"Don't take them all. Leave some for your mother."

When Louise got back, she found them hard at it, and, as if she didn't know, they greeted her gaily with the news:

"We're going."

It was Henri who pleaded:

"Let's go to Paris, Mother. I want to get a job on a newspaper, and I'd have a better chance there than anywhere else."

"We're going to Poitiers."

"Why Poitiers?"

"Because there's an apartment for us there."

She came up to tell Jeanne all about it. She too seemed to have burst the bonds that had attached her to this house and already to be moving about it as though she didn't really belong there.

"As luck would have it, Cousin Marthe was actually delighted by what has happened. She never liked the Martineau family, and now she's proved right. She kept on saying:

" 'I knew it would end up like this. I always told your father so.'

"Thanks to that, I got more out of her than I expected. Particularly when I told her about Robert's double life."

"You told her that?"

But Jeanne understood very well that Louise had only done so because it was good policy.

"She offered me an apartment that happens to be vacant at the moment in one of her houses in Poitiers. She owns almost a whole street. It's in a working-class area near the railway, but that's better than nothing. The one thing that really scared me was the thought of finding myself in the street."

"Will you have to pay rent?"

"Oh, yes. But not until we get straightened out."

"Did she let you have some money?"

"A little."

She didn't say how much, preferring not to be too precise, which made Jeanne think she had got considerably more than the two or three thousand francs she had been expecting that morning. This was now her money, and she was going to take good care of it.

"The children seem quite pleased about it."

"They're treating it as a picnic. Henri's only regret is the car."

"Have you come to any decision yourself?"

"I must talk to Dr. Bernard first."

"When's he coming?"

"In the morning."

"I told my cousin we'd leave before midday tomorrow, to be out of the place before the sheriff's man comes, when, of course, the news will be all over town in a flash. I'd better go and start packing myself now. Is there anything you want?"

They hadn't gone to bed till late at night, and it must have seemed strange to passers-by to see the lights on in all the windows. Désirée had already studied the want ads in the local paper, and she slipped out for an hour to answer one for a cook.

"I'm starting tomorrow afternoon," she told Jeanne on her return. "It doesn't seem a bad place, though the lady's almost stone deaf. Are you going with them?"

"I don't know, Désirée. For the moment, they're on the crest of the wave. In a couple of days, when they've had a few floors to scrub, a few meals to cook, and the washing up to do, they'll be singing a different tune. By the way, I haven't seen Alice or the baby."

"Monsieur Fisolle came for them. Alice called him up. He must have taken a taxi or begged the use of a friend's car; I heard one draw up at the house. He didn't come in and didn't say a word to anybody—just stood on the doorstep waiting for her. She had to carry everything down herself. I don't think she said good-bye to a soul. Anyhow, it's good riddance! . . . What would you like to eat this evening?"

Later on, when she had finished the dishes, Désirée came up again to sit by Jeanne and chat for a while before going to bed.

"Do your legs hurt?"

"Not when I'm lying down, and so long as I keep warm. They just feel like two great lumps of lead."

"Of course, if you haven't any money saved or any pension, you haven't much choice but to go and live with them. But I'm sorry for you. It'll be worse than being a servant. As soon as you're on your feet again they'll leave all the work to you. And if you fall ill again—you'll see—it won't be long before they'll be grudging you the bread you eat, and making you feel it. I've seen enough of them in these few days to know. Besides, it's always like that. My mother-in-law, who had money tucked away in every corner, knew what she was about when she made up her mind she wasn't going to be dependent on anybody. A good thing for her she did, because her husband spent every sou he could lay his hands on and didn't leave her a bean."

She felt herself to be on equal terms with Jeanne now and took full advantage of it. In fact, their roles were almost reversed, for it was her future that seemed the more secure of the two.

"Have you been to the hotel to pay your bill?"

"No. And I must confess I'd forgotten about it."

"You know, if I was in your place, I'd try to get into one of those institutions. There are some where you're very well looked after."

She had avoided calling it a workhouse.

"At least you're not dependent on anyone that way. I can't see you working for others."

"I'll think about it, Désirée."

"You must have had a queer life. Lots of ups and downs, I suppose."

"Yes."

"Is it true Lauer never married you?"

"Who told you that?"

"I heard the children talking about it. I was quite taken aback. They must have heard it from their mother."

"Who got it from the notary," added Jeanne. "News travels fast. Yes, it's quite true."

"Why? Didn't he love you? I thought you'd stayed together right up to his death?"

"We lived together. The thing was—he was already married."

"So he'd left his wife? Why did he do that?"

"He said it had been a mistake. He didn't attach any great importance to marriage. Nor did I. It wasn't for the sake of getting married that I left home."

"But you knew, when you went, that you were going to live with him?"

"I'd have gone anyhow."

"What would you have done?"

"Anything. I wanted to be on my own. I was proud."

"You still are, aren't you?"

"Do you think so? It's possible. Proud or very humble. Perhaps it comes to much the same thing. I met Lauer when he was on a holiday, staying with his aunt."

"He was a lot older than you, wasn't he?"

"Not that much. Ten years. He wrote for newspapers and was interested in all sorts of things. He was a clever man and very cultured."

"Why did you go to South America?"

"He had an offer and jumped at it. One evening in a bar, somebody suggested he should go as editor of a newspaper that was being launched by a group of exporters. He didn't think twice about it, and we sailed a week later with just about enough money to last us till we got to Buenos Aires, where we were to get more. Does this amuse you?"

"I had imagined your life quite differently."

"Yes, there were ups and downs. The newspaper scheme

fell through, and for a while we lived on next to nothing in a filthy little hotel, wondering whether we wouldn't have to apply to the consulate for repatriation. But finally Lauer did manage to get a paper started. A political paper. Then there was the business of the fifteen thousand rifles.

"At that time, not only the governments of South America but all the political parties were always in quest of arms. When it wasn't a war they wanted, it was a revolution. That meant good business for arms merchants. Provided, of course, you could deliver the goods. That was the difficulty. Someone, again in a bar—for we spent the best part of our time in hotels and bars—someone told Lauer he had fifteen thousand rifles in a ship lying in some port or other, I can't remember which. And he offered him a huge commission if he could sell them.

"The trouble was to get them from one place to another, since there were always all sorts of regulations to get around.

"Still, we sold them. I say 'we,' because I played my part too."

"What makes you laugh?"

"It was a comic-opera business. Very funny when you come to look back on it. Funny and deplorable at the same time. We never saw those rifles. In fact, they may never have existed. Yet we sold them, not once, but over and over again. We lived very well on them, sometimes luxuriously. The ship they were in, or supposed to be in, flew the Greek flag. It sailed up and down the coast from Panama to Tierra del Fuego, without ever being able to unload.

"We'd get our commission, and then at the last minute something would crop up, a storm, a revolution, or trouble with the police."

"Do you mean Lauer arranged it on purpose?"

"Very possibly. For a while we were received in grand style by ministers and generals, until the day arrived when it was advisable for us to get a change of air! Without a moment's delay! And we got out just in time to avoid being thrown in jail or even shot. For helping rebels. That was the funny thing, since we'd helped nobody.

"We reached Havana, where Lauer, who had nothing if not style, managed to get on the right side of the French minister, who took him under his wing. For everybody, I was Madame Lauer. There was talk of founding another paper, or this time, a magazine. To boost French culture in all the states of Latin America."

"You had to leave?"

"For Cairo. Without even taking our luggage, because we owed I don't know how many weeks' room and board at our hotel."

"You didn't mind living like that?"

"It's the life I had chosen."

"Did you still love him?"

Jeanne looked at her, and avoided giving a direct answer.

"You see, I knew him so well," she said. "I knew all his faults and failings, and God knows he had his fair share."

"Did you point them out to him?"

"Yes."

"You quarreled?"

"Almost every night. And he'd end by knocking me around."

"You let him do that?"

"Sometimes I even provoked it deliberately."

"I can't understand that."

"It doesn't matter. I had run away; don't forget that. And, when one begins to degenerate, it's sometimes a pleasure to plunge in on purpose deeper and deeper."

"As if I'd taken to being a servant just for the fun of it!"

"If you like."

"You couldn't have loved him, yet you stuck to him and obeyed him like a dog."

"Yes. And then we used to drink together, particularly toward the end of his life. We'd spend the best part of the night drinking, finishing up with a quarrel. Then he was taken to the hospital with pleurisy and died in three weeks."

"Leaving you nothing, I suppose. Was it then you started working for those Belgians?"

"Soon after. Not at once."

She reddened and sheered away from the subject. If she'd tried to earn a living in other ways, she preferred not to speak about it, not even to think of it.

"You'd better be off to bed now, Désirée. That's all. You tried pretty hard to worm it out of me, and I owed it to you to satisfy your curiosity. You've done me a good turn. And when you think of me you can always say that whatever happened to me was of my own seeking, so there's no need to shed any tears over it."

Before leaving, Désirée, who had been ruminating for a minute or two, turned in the doorway to say with a sigh:

"I see you're one of the family, all right!"

"Come in, Doctor. And would you mind shutting the door? I may have some questions to ask you that there's no need for anyone else to hear. It's a long time since you've seen such life in the house, isn't it?"

"Are you going with them?" he asked as he pulled down the covers.

"I want to know first what you think of my legs. The swelling's gone down a bit since yesterday, and they're turning a little blue. Just now I managed to hobble all by myself to the bathroom."

He pressed here and there with his finger, making white patches which he watched slowly disappear, his forehead puckered.

"I must examine your heart thoroughly."

He was at it for a good ten minutes. He didn't use a stethoscope but, spreading a washcloth over her chest, put his ear against it. Then he listened with his ear against her back.

"Well, Doctor?"

"You were right. There's not much wrong with it. I don't think there's any need for an electrocardiogram."

"Why do you look so worried?"

"I asked you what you intended to do. I hear your sister-in-law and the children are leaving for Poitiers this morning."

146

"They are. And I'm in no shape for traveling, am I?"

"Certainly not under the present circumstances, with nothing ready at the other end. And, since you can't stay here either, I'll have you moved to the hospital as soon as possible."

He watched her, expecting her to bristle at the word "hospital," to protest, or even to weep. But she went on smiling at him.

"Sit down for a moment, Doctor."

"I've got a lot of patients to see this morning. I'm afraid I can't stay many minutes."

"Yet it's you who've been wanting to ask me questions, ever since Sunday morning. You haven't done so for fear of offending me or hurting my feelings. Perhaps also because you think you've no business to pry into your patients' private lives. . . . To start the ball rolling, let me ask you a precise question: supposing, when I'm on my feet again, I start working as I have been these last few days, how long will it be before the trouble flares up again?"

"A few weeks at the most."

"And after that?"

"You'll go to bed for a while, then go back to work till you're driven back to bed again. And it'll happen more and more frequently. Particularly in the summer."

"About half the time in bed and half up?"

"Not so much as that. Not at first."

"Later on?"

"It'll get worse with the years."

"How many years before I'm completely infirm?"

"It depends on how much you take care of yourself. If you go with them, I would say four or five. On the other hand . . ."

"Yes. Go on."

"If you don't go with them, I wonder what will become of those two children."

"What would you do in my place?"

"I'd rather not answer that, if you don't mind."

"So it comes to this: I'm in rather the same predicament as my brother. Monsieur Bigeois was speaking to us this morning of his three possible solutions. I've got three too. There's the infirmary, where I can live in peace, at any rate, and have my legs looked after. There's the family, in which I shall be a slave one week and a fearful burden to everyone the next."

"Exactly."

"I needn't mention the third."

"No."

"I think the old lawyer disapproved of the course Robert took."

"He hoped for something else."

"That he'd bolt. I know. And you?"

"Monsieur Bigeois and I don't necessarily see eye to eye."

"You think Robert was right?"

"I'm a Catholic."

"Which means that he should have gone to prison. And now, what is it to be for me? The infirmary?"

"As a doctor, that's what I'm bound to advise."

"But as a man and a Catholic you'd rather see me devote what strength I have left to keeping the family together."

"You could."

"Yes. With a lot of care and a certain amount of guile, I could probably prevent them from tearing each other to bits, and themselves into the bargain. I can keep Louise off drink, at any rate for a time, and above all prevent her from making those dreadful scenes that put everybody on the rack. Who knows? I might even in the long run get Henri to resign himself to being a little clerk, content to be an ordinary person. That's the part you see me playing, isn't it? And I might wheedle Mad into marrying a decent boy without flinging all her past misdeeds in his face. Little by little, Louise will come to detest me, but will make the best of me rather than do the washing up herself or having the children screaming at her. Also for fear of being left alone one day. And it won't be long before the children regret having confided in me and even bear me a grudge for it, though that won't stop them running to me again when they want to unburden themselves or make themselves interesting.

"I shall be Aunt Jeanne, the beast of burden, first up, last to bed, to whom there's nothing that can't be said, from whom there's nothing that can't be asked, and who always remains just the same. And later on, if Henri or Mad have children . . ."

"I'm afraid I must be going. . . ."

"And I don't mind betting last Saturday Monsieur Bigeois cut short my brother's speech too. But don't be afraid. That's not a threat."

"My job is to heal the sick."

"I know. But now and again you give them a discreet but inquisitive glance out of the corner of your eye, because you can't get away from the fact that they're men and women all the same."

"I'll get the ambulance to call for you toward the end of the morning. We'll come back to this subject in the hospital."

"What? In a public ward? You don't imagine I can pay for a private one, do you?"

He grasped the doorknob, then paused.

"In any case . . ." he began.

But he pulled himself up.

"No. I don't want to influence you one way or the other. I'll be seeing you there."

"I'd have been only too glad to stay behind to look after you, Jeanne. But you know the situation as well as I do. I'm afraid the hospital's the only solution. But you must promise me you'll join us when you're well again. I'll put our address in your bag. There's no telephone. Just send a telegram, and Henri will come to meet you at the station, which is only just around the corner."

Mad kissed her aunt on the cheek and whispered in her ear:

"You'll come, won't you? For my sake."

"Good-bye, Aunt Jeanne," said Henri, looking through

the window at the truck that was driving off with their possessions.

A moment later, Désirée appeared.

"Well, that's cleared the house a bit," she said with a sigh of relief. "As for what's left, I suppose you could say it belongs to nobody. To think of all that stuff being auctioned off! Why, it must have cost a small fortune. Tomorrow they'll come nosing around, prying into every corner, to take their inventory. I know all about that. When we were auctioned off, I stayed right to the end. I even watched the sale. There were heaps of people there, though of course lots of them didn't come to buy anything, but just to look."

"What's Monsieur Sallenave say?"

"He mopes about like a dog that's lost its master. And he goes on worrying over his books as though it was a matter of life and death that every franc should be accounted for. . . . And what about you? Have you made up your mind yet?"

"Not quite."

"Don't you go with them. Any institution, even the worst, would be better than that. Don't listen to the doctor."

"How do you know what Dr. Bernard thinks?"

"It was written all over his face. I know that type of man. I could take my oath there's not a speck of dust anywhere in his house and that his maid doesn't get one evening off in a week."

"Désirée!"

"What is it?"

"You remember that cupboard?"

"With the bottles?"

"Yes."

"What of it?"

"Louise has probably forgotten about those bottles. You said there were three full ones. Now, don't ask me why, and don't preach me a sermon."

"You want me to . . ."

"Yes. To bring one up to me. You needn't bother about a glass. The one I use for my teeth will do."

150

"You really want me to do that?"

"Yes."

"What'll they say at the hospital when you arrive with your breath smelling of drink?"

"Go on! They're used to it."

"You insist?"

"I insist. And there's nothing for you to be afraid of."

She smiled strangely as she listened to Désirée's steps on the stairs.

"Give it to me. I'll open it. I'm more used to opening corks than you are. Get me my glass from the bathroom."

Her old schoolfellow watched her uncork the bottle. She was shocked and pained, though not altogether surprised, after what Jeanne had told her of her life.

At first she had thought Jeanne a marvel, but that was all over now.

"Aren't you putting any water with it?"

It wasn't a pretty sight, this fat woman sitting up in bed gulping down mouthful after mouthful of brandy, which scorched her chest and brought on a violent fit of coughing. Unable to stop, she made Désirée a sign to pat her back. Finally the rasping cough finished with a groan, followed by a sigh, after which Jeanne's face instantly recovered its strange smile.

"That's better."

"Won't you be drunk?"

"I don't know. Why?"

"Perhaps that's what you want."

Jeanne didn't answer. And a little later, with the same expression on her face, an expression in which smug contentment was mixed with caustic contempt, she remarked:

"It's about time I came to a decision, isn't it?"

"You're not going to follow your brother's example, are you?"

"No. That's just the point."

Her face was flushed and her watery eyes sparkled.

"And I think it's not going to be the infirmary either."

She was discussing the matter with herself. Désirée had faded into the background, a vague black-and-white figure standing in the sunshine.

"You people are altogether too complicated for me."

"Listen."

"I'm listening all right. Only I don't want to miss the ambulance, which may be here at any moment now."

"I'll go and join them in a week or so, as soon as I'm on my feet again. In fact, I don't mind betting it'll be inside a week."

"The truth is you're like everyone else. You're afraid of being alone, aren't you?"

"It's not that."

"Afraid of dying, then."

Jeanne went on smiling, and it exasperated Désirée, who was sorely tempted to be disagreeable.

"You're too proud to go to an institution."

"Don't be silly."

"So you want to make out it's all for their sake."

"It's not at all certain I'll do them any good. I think I'm just beginning to understand what the lawyer said this morning. He's lived longer than I have. There are people who go up and people who go down, there are people who go this way and people who go that. There isn't such an awful lot we can do about it."

"We do our best," answered Désirée tartly, as though these observations had been a reflection upon her.

"Yes. We do our best. That's just about what I meant. We try to make peace with ourselves."

"Do you feel at peace now?"

"I did when I was rushing up and down stairs with Bob in my arms, when I was struggling to keep the whole house going, to avoid a catastrophe."

"It wasn't much use, was it? Like your scrubbing floors up to midnight after the funeral!"

"How do you know?"

"It's the same as it was with Lauer, isn't it? You do it to . . ."

". . . to get up first in the morning and make the coffee, so that all's in order when the others come down. To be up to my elbows in soapy water, so that the house is clean and inviting. Only to find, when I'm nearly dropping with fatigue, that there's still more to do, that the work is never finished. And in the end to crawl up to bed, expecting never to get up from it again, and then, instead of going to sleep, to lie thinking of all that has to be done next day."

"To be a slave, in fact. If you'd been in service as long as I have. you'd know more about things. And a lot more about people!"

"It isn't so much the people that count. It's . . ."

She filled her glass again and contemplated it with a sort of melancholy joy.

"It's all right. This is the last. I thought I'd have just one more, and . . ."

She took a sip, then calmly threw the glass to the floor.

"As you say, the house belongs to nobody now, so there's no need for you to wipe it up. . . . Isn't that the ambulance?"

"Shall I sent them up?"

"Yes. Send them right up. Don't worry. I'll be on my best behavior. They'll be a bit surprised at the smell of brandy in here, no doubt, but once I'm in the hospital I shall be a model patient and be a great favorite with everyone. And, because I'll do all they tell me, I'll be out again in a few days. Then Poitiers. Yes, I'll go to them. I'll be their Aunt Jeanne. . . . I've got enough money left for the fare."

Désirée went out shrugging her shoulders. Left alone, Jeanne smiled no longer. In fact, she looked scared as she listened to the men's footsteps and the stretcher bumping against the wall.

Her hands clutched the sheet, as though at the last moment she wanted, after all, to cling to this house, to this room that had been hers long ago, to the little chest of drawers between the windows.

"Aunt Jeanne," she murmured, as though rehearsing a new part.

Two great louts stood over her, inspecting her, as though

estimating her weight. She saw them exchange winks, before she closed her eyes. Then she heard the dark one say:

"Ready, Jean?"

And the cheery answer:

"Yes. Here she goes!"